I0652479

DREAM OF A SUMMER NIGHT

BY THE SAME AUTHOR

Yemen Rediscovered (*Longman*)
Bahrain: Gulf Heritage in Transition (*Longman*)
Syria in View (*Longman*)
Scotland through the Ages (*Michael Joseph*)
London Heritage (*Michael Joseph*)
Traveller's Companion to the West Country (*Michael Joseph*)
Journeys into Medieval England (*Michael Joseph*)
Ireland through the Ages (*Michael Joseph*)
Architectural Heritage of Britain & Ireland (*Michael Joseph*)
Victorian Britain (*Weidenfeld & Nicolson*)
New British Architecture in Germany (*Prestel*)
FlipDesigns (*Prestel*)
FlipSigns (*Prestel*)
Mrs Mulroony's Fly-Away French Bloomers (*Lulu*)
Off Course (*Lulu*)
Conundrum's Book (*Lulu*)
Farthing Abbey (*Lulu*)

DREAM OF A SUMMER NIGHT

Michael Jenner

ISBN 978-0-9558480-3-2
© Michael Jenner, 2008

For Diana, the love of my life.

EAR TO THE DOOR

Tom has been woken by a phone ringing. Unable to sleep he goes downstairs. Through the closed door of the living room he overhears voices. His parents are talking. He stops to listen.

"I can't believe it."

"Can't believe what?"

"That phone call."

"Phone call?"

"You'll never guess."

"Guess what?"

"Fabulous news."

"News? What news?"

"It's Africa."

"Africa?"

"Yes, Africa. A two month field research trip. Up the Limpopo. Down the Congo. All the places I've ever dreamed of visiting."

He'd never heard Dad get so excited.

"And do you know the best bit?"

"Well I won't unless you tell me."

With one ear pressed tight against the keyhole Tom strains to catch every word.

"You can come too. Isn't that brilliant?"

There follows a long heavy pause before at last Mum speaks.

"But that's completely out of the question."

Yet another long pause before Mum continues.

"Aren't you overlooking something?"

"Something?"

"Or rather someone."

"Someone?"

The penny finally drops for Dad.

"You mean Tom?"

"Young Tom. Yes, indeed. We do have our one and only son to look after. If you haven't forgotten."

He is on the point of bursting in to tell them they needn't worry about him. He'd come too. Really he would. Nothing he'd like better than to go with them to Africa. Up the Limpopo. Down the Congo. Wherever, whatever. But if he did burst in right now, they'd know he'd been eavesdropping. After all, it's late and he's meant to be in bed, not wandering about the house in his pyjamas. On the other hand, it's not his fault the phone has woken him up, and now he's wide-awake he might just as well listen in. No harm in that, surely?

"Well, I suppose I could ask the expedition organisers about taking Tom with us?"

Yes! Yes!! Yes!!!

He wants to hug Dad for this brilliant idea.

"But Africa is far too dangerous for a young boy. All those poisonous snakes and wild animals."

Why on earth do you have to raise such stupid objections, Mum? Africa must be full of African kids. Surely it must be just as dangerous for them.

"Let's be honest, Tom's not very grown up for his age. All his friends are out riding their mountain

10

bikes or doing clever stuff on computers, and he prefers sitting about chatting to that battered old teddy bear."

What a thing to say, Mum. Not fair. Not fair at all.

Anyway, that battered old teddy bear has a name. He's called Arthur, and Tom owes Arthur, owes him a lot as it happens. He and Arthur have been through it all together. The rough and the smooth. The thick and the thin. Much else besides. Things you can't expect parents to understand. He can't just dump Arthur simply because Mum and Dad have decided it's time for him to grow up.

"But we've got to face facts. Tom's really not ready for somewhere like Africa. He's too timid by half. Frightened of new challenges, I reckon."

Frightened? Hold on, Mum. Just because I prefer Arthur's company to nerdy computer games or fooling around on a silly old mountain bike, that doesn't mean I'm scared of new challenges and stuff.

"Yes, I suppose you do have a point. Tom isn't very enterprising. Perhaps he's a late developer?"

Hey, Dad! Not you too?

"Well he won't develop much if he hasn't given up reading those picture stories with talking animals we gave him all those years ago. They still have pride of place on the shelf above his bed, you know."

That's right out of order. Just because I haven't thrown away my old books, it doesn't mean I'm still reading them.

"I don't know where Tom gets that immature streak from. Certainly not from my side of the family."

"Not from my side either."

Is this what his parents really think of him? He feels a sudden rush of tears. Now to cap it all, he is going to cry. That will only serve to prove them right. Last thing he wants. So he takes a deep breath and clenches his eyelids tightly shut. By some miracle he keeps the floodgates closed.

Perhaps he should go back to bed? But he remains standing there in the hall, rooted to the spot, ear still glued to the living room door. It has never occurred to him Mum and Dad could have anything but the nicest things to say about him. And here they are agreeing he isn't brave or grown up. Well, let them say what they want. He would hear the worst.

"So what shall we do with him then? We'll be away for the whole of the summer holidays."

"Yes, that's a big problem."

But it couldn't have been such a big problem. Because only a couple of seconds pass before Tom's Mum squeals with delight.

"I've got it. Listen to this. We'll send Tom to stay with great-uncle Percy in Oxford while we're away. That will be perfect. Absolutely perfect."

Great-uncle Percy? Surely not?.

"You don't mean that crusty old professor?"

"Who else?"

"You can't be serious. He's a dry old stick. What on earth will the two of them have in common?"

"Precisely my point. Since we are both agreed Tom needs to grow up, and it doesn't seem to be happening at home, so perhaps a little bit of great-uncle Percy's mature wisdom might do the trick."

It seems like Mum's mind is made up, well and truly. He now listens hard to what Dad will say. He knows it is his last hope.

"But your great-uncle Percy is more than mature. He's ancient. Practically a fossil. He should really be in a glass case in one of those museums where he spends most of his time. Shouldn't Tom be with someone more his own age?"

Go on, Dad. That's the stuff. You tell her!

"That's just it. With great-uncle Percy Tom will learn to behave in a proper grown-up manner."

His heart sinks. Mum is clearly determined to have her way. But although it is now a lost cause, Dad doesn't give up altogether.

"But how do you suppose they'll communicate? The only time they met, Tom was very small, and all your great-uncle Percy could say when he saw him was *Cripes!* - as if he'd never seen a child before."

Cripes? What's that supposed to mean?

"But that was ages ago. They'll get on ok. Just as long as Tom puts childish things behind him. Beginning with that battered old teddy bear. He can't take it with him, you know. Tell you what, we'll stick Arthur in the attic while Tom's away. I bet he'll never even miss him when he gets back. You'll see."

Mum really seems to have it in for Arthur. As if he were to blame. Dad blusters on for a bit. But to no avail. It's all done and dusted. The entire summer holidays with great-uncle Percy in Oxford while his parents swan about in Africa.

Cripes! And double cripes!!

Tom creeps back upstairs. What really hurts most is not being left behind, though that's bad enough, but that his parents have such a wrong idea about him. And he can think of nothing to put them right. Nothing, nothing, nothing. The word runs through his head in an endless loop as he places his feet carefully one after the other on the stairs so they won't creak.

Through some curious magic, by the time he reaches his bedroom door that nothing has become a something. It has formed itself into a cunning plan. A perfect plan. A nothing plan. He would do nothing, say nothing. Absolutely nothing. Even less than nothing if that were possible. He will accept his fate without a murmur. He will make no fuss, shed no tears, play no tantrums. In fact, showing nothing would show them good and proper. It won't be easy but he feels he can do it. The toughest part would be breaking it to dear old Arthur he was going to be left behind.

NO WAY BACK

Next morning, Tom's parents waste no time announcing their good news about Africa and then the bad news about Tom staying with great-uncle Percy in Oxford. Of course, they don't put it to him just like that. It is all wrapped up with lots of fine sugary words. To listen to them you might think they are the ones who have the raw deal, having to go on some tiresome expedition.

When they have finished, they wait for their son's reaction. Tight-lipped, Tom sticks to his nothing plan. He simply nods to show he has understood. When finally pressed to say something further, he astounds them and even himself.

"Africa, ace. Up the Limpopo, lovely. Down the Congo, cool. You have a great time. I'll be OK with great-uncle Percy in Oxford. No worries."

They can hardly believe their ears. Not a word of protest. They dare not question their son further in case he says something they don't want to hear. As for Tom, he draws a tiny bit of comfort from his success in pulling the wool over their eyes. But this small triumph leaves him curiously empty.

After that, the days and weeks slide by slowly with nothing much said about their separate plans for the summer holidays. Then on the fateful day when he is to be taken away, Tom almost loses it at the last moment when he says farewell to Arthur.

"See you soon, old pal."

But it won't be soon. More like never. With heavy heart he shuts his bedroom door and follows his parents out to the car.

When they reach the outskirts of Oxford Tom comes over all quiet. Putting a brave face on things is getting tougher by the mile. Mum and Dad really are about to dump him on great-uncle Percy and fly off to Africa. The hand-over actually takes place on the doorstep. He might just as well be a package delivered to the wrong address. For great-uncle Percy looks at him with an extremely puzzled expression.

"Cripes! And who are you, young man? Should I be expecting you?"

Then the old man recognises Tom's parents who are hovering behind on the garden path.

"Oh it's you. Of course. So this must be young Tom. That's right, isn't it? Said I'd look after him, didn't I? Sorry I can't ask you in for tea. Frightfully busy right now. And I'm sure you don't want to miss your plane. So let me wish you a successful expedition to Africa."

Tom says nothing, his courage all used up. He fears he will blab like a baby if he looks Mum and Dad in the eye. So he just stares obstinately at the ground.

Parents, who needs them?

A couple of quick hugs and kisses and then they are gone. A vast emptiness swallows him up. Tom is all alone with great-uncle Percy. The old man stares at him intently in a way he's never been stared at before. As if the old man has seen something for the first time in his life. Then he seems to lose interest. No sooner has he ushered Tom inside the house than he heads straight for the study, sits down at a writing desk, grabs a sheet of paper and begins scribbling feverishly.

Tom sits numb with gloom on a rickety wooden chair in the corner, while the old man fills page after page with his messy writing. After what seems an eternity, he puts down his pen, breathes a deep sigh and rises to his feet. As an afterthought, he remembers Tom and beckons him to follow. They are going out.

But 'going out' is great-uncle Percy wobbling along on a rusty old bike stuck in second gear with Tom running behind as fast as he can all the way for the couple of miles into the centre of Oxford. Here the growing up plan cleverly hatched by Tom's parents is about to go wrong. Badly wrong.

Great-uncle Percy takes Tom into a gift shop tucked away inside an ancient stone building. At the far end there are shelves laden with teddy bears of every imaginable shape and size.

"Now how do you think we're going to keep you occupied, young man?"

Tom shrugs his shoulders.

"I'll buy you a teddy bear!"

Tom is alarmed.

"No, please don't do that."

"Why ever not?"

His parents would be hopping mad.

"I don't want one."

"You don't want a teddy bear?"

"Actually, I'm too old for bears."

"Too old for bears? Stuff and nonsense. You're never too old for bears. And I'll buy you two if you don't stop making such a fuss."

Tom bites his tongue and settles for just the one. He feels guilty twice over. First, for going against his parents' wishes. Second, for betraying Arthur whose place is now to be taken by an unknown impostor. As a result Tom doesn't give the new bear a second glance. He decides he won't even unwrap it.

When they arrive back home Tom is again left to his own devices for hours on end while great-uncle Percy carries on with his tall mountain of paperwork as if all alone in a world of his own.

"Just go and play with that handsome new bear of yours, young man."

That said, Tom is again ignored by great-uncle Percy. Dinnertime comes and goes. Nothing to eat. He is eventually offered a dry biscuit and a glass of lukewarm milk that tastes a bit cheesy. Shortly after that he trudges upstairs to his room at the very top of the house right under the sloping roof. Well, to be honest it is hardly a room in the proper sense, just a rickety camp bed squeezed into a poky space surrounded by piles of dusty old books. That night, homesick and hungry, he lies awake full of gloomy thoughts. How can he survive two days let alone two whole months of this?

At least, if he had brought Arthur with him, there would be someone to talk to. But talking to bears is childish and he is supposed to be growing up, isn't he?

That's the whole point of his being here, isn't it? But old habits die hard. In the dark he can just make out the package containing the new bear great-uncle Percy bought him. There's no one else to talk to, so why not? Surely it won't hurt just to take a peek? Arthur would understand. Of course he would.

Tom slips out of bed, picks up the unopened package and carries it to the window. By the light of the pale yellow moon he removes the paper wrapping. No sooner does he look into the coal-black eyes staring out at him than everything starts to go fuzzy at the edges. Tom thinks he is passing out. But instead he dissolves into thin air, vanishing like a genie from a lamp, leaving behind no trace. He simply isn't there anymore, and next morning he still isn't there either.

Under normal circumstances, there would have been a news flash on TV. Missing boy. Massive police search. Shocked parents making tearful public appeal. Posters of young Tom put up in phone boxes and shop windows. But there is none of that. For there aren't any shocked parents on hand to report his absence. By now they are thousands of miles away in Africa.

Next morning great-uncle Percy does not notice his great-nephew is absent. Sure enough, he suspects he might have overlooked something or other. But the absent-minded professor is always forgetting something or other. So what is the difference between a missing book and a missing great-nephew, especially if you have no clear memory of either?

We'll wish young Tom good luck, wherever he is. But now the scene changes. Not too far away in actual distance, but so remote in every other respect, as if on a distant planet or in a parallel universe, something weird and wonderful is happening. A new life is poised to begin, wide-eyed as a fluffy chick pecking its way out of an egg. Only it's not a bird, but a being of another species altogether. Strange things are afoot in the middle of this mysterious midsummer Oxford night.

CRIPES!

He pinched himself once then twice to make quite sure he wasn't dreaming. No, he wasn't, unless this was a new kind of dream.

"Cripes! What's going on?"

He had no clue where he was. What's more, he couldn't recall ever having said *Cripes!* before. It wasn't the kind of word he used. Really it wasn't. Not like him at all. On the other hand, he didn't know what was like him. In fact, he had no idea who he was. But that particular thought hadn't yet occurred to him. Peering into the darkness, he could dimly make out postcards, china mugs, dinner mats and assorted knick-knacks, mostly decorated with olde worlde views of medieval spires and cloisters.

"What on earth am I doing here?"

On either side, he saw a long row of teddy bears wearing blue vests adorned with a motto in something foreign he couldn't quite make out.

"How very odd. Can't imagine how I got mixed up with this little lot."

He scratched his head. It felt furrier than usual. Curious. He was sure it had been somehow different before. Before? Before what? But he couldn't recall a thing about *before*. The past simply didn't exist. As for the present, he was completely in the dark about that too. For a start, where was he?

Leaning forward to get a better view he lost his balance and came tumbling down from a high shelf. By good fortune a pile of tea towels cushioned his fall. He picked himself up and looked about. A ghostly stone archway beckoned him into a cavernous room spooky as a crypt where skeletons are stored. He beat a hasty retreat. Next, he climbed a crooked wooden staircase that creaked and groaned beneath his feet. He reached a landing. A sign announced Duke Humfrey's Library. He pushed open the door. The room was full of tall bookcases standing smartly to attention like sentry boxes. Nothing stirred. No sign of the Duke.

He slipped inside and crept over to a window, scrambling up onto a gnarled oak desktop to peep outside. His eyes widened at a magical moon-drenched scene of steeples, towers and gargoyles all spread out under a sky of deep indigo blue. Moonlight filtered through the glass panes onto the spines of stout leather volumes that glinted and gleamed with gold titles.

Suddenly, he felt tired, so very tired. An empty space yawned where a book was missing. So he crawled inside and made himself snug. As he lay there he listened to the steady tick-tock of a grandfather clock. It counted each and every second like big silver coins dropping one by one into a treasure chest.

He was about to drop off to sleep, when he became aware of two large, luminous, green eyes staring at him out of a huge book. He blinked to make sure he wasn't imagining things. No, he wasn't. The green eyes blinked back, magnified alarmingly by thick spectacles.

"Permit me to introduce myself. Victor Verum. *Servitum vostrum*[1], bookworm in residence, and you?"

"Well, er ..."

"A bit tongue-tied, are we? No matter. I shall call you Bodley. After the Bodleian Library, of course. Naming lost bears after the place where they are found is standard practice, don't you know?"

"Lost bears? I may be lost. But surely not a lost bear? There must be some mistake?"

Bodley – as he had now been officially renamed by Victor Verum – looked closely at his hands. They were more like paws. In fact, they were paws. Cripes! So he was a bear! How odd, how very odd. That was not how he remembered himself. Trouble was he couldn't really remember himself as being anything else either. He searched in vain for even a hazy memory of who or what he might once have been.

Victor Verum eyed him with interest.

"What a curious fellow you are, my dear Bodley."

He looked at the tiny bookworm in amazement. A talking bookworm? But before he could even think straight, Victor Verum was talking again.

"Don't look so surprised. Eating books is not as bad as all that. I tend to go for the useless stuff, and there's plenty of that in here. Working nights isn't my idea of fun. All Mildew's fault really. Head Librarian. The big cheese. Always on the prowl during the day.

---

[1] Rough translation: "Victor Worm, your servant."

Soon as I've got a book between my teeth, he charges in like a mad bull and snatches it away. *Olé! Olé! Olé!* Pretty spiffing, my Spanish, don't you reckon?"

"Well, er..."

"Foreign lingos are my speciality as it happens. I've dined on dozens of delicious dialects over the years. Want a demo?"

"Well, er..."

"Now I bet you enjoy a good old gossip in Greek, don't you?"

"Well, er ..."

"*Mega. Alpha plus.* Or do you prefer a jolly old jabber in German?"

"Well, er ..."

"*Wunderbar.* I once had a nibble at the Berlin phonebook. Not that tasty, but very filling. *Danke schön.* So what do you say to that?"

"Well, er ..."

"But you can't beat French for being seriously silly, *n'est-ce pas?*"

"Well, er ..."

"*Exactement.*"

Bodley was flabbergasted. Just how many languages could Victor Verum speak? Then he had a bright idea. Surely, this ever-so-clever bookworm could tell him what he was doing here, and perhaps even who he was? He would put the question as soon as he could get a word in edgeways. But Victor Verum's velvety voice droned on and on. Very hypnotic it was too. Before long Bodley nodded off. However, this made not the slightest difference to the talkative bookworm who continued to speak volumes.

Finally, Victor Verum paused for breath.

"Well enough of that. Let's hear what you have to say for yourself. Any questions? If there's anything you want to know, just ask away. I'm clued up on pretty well everything you can think of. *Servitum vostrum* only too pleased to oblige etc etc."

This was Bodley's chance to ask all the questions he wanted. But now he was fast asleep, completely out for the count. Nothing could rouse him. Seeing this, the bookworm gave out a sad little sigh and carried on munching his way deeper and deeper into the big book right above Bodley's sleeping head until he had completely vanished from view.

But Victor Verum remained in Bodley's mind. For much of the night, his restless dreams were haunted by a pair of large, green bespectacled eyes that watched over him while the long, dark shadows of Duke Humfrey's men stalked through the moonlit library in search of an intruder. Eventually, his fears dissolved and for the rest of the night he slept as soundly as any bear in a warm cave snuggled up among his nearest and dearest. He dozed on until just after the grandfather clock chimed nine in the morning.

At the final chime an almighty explosion rocked Bodley out of his slumbers. He awoke to the sight of a big, red handkerchief quivering from the aftershock of a powerful sneeze. A couple of seconds passed before another almighty explosion rattled the windows. After a third blast, the sneezer put away the big, red handkerchief and revealed himself. He was an old man. A cascade of white hair fell almost to his shoulders. To Bodley's young eyes, he looked incredibly ancient.

"Blasted nuisance this ha … ha …. hay fee … ee … eever …. aa … aaa … atishoo! Bless me! Never gave me any trouble in the desert. No pollen out there. This perishing place is full of the dreadful stuff."

It seemed the old man was talking to himself. His mumbled words were clearly not addressed to Bodley. Was this Duke Humfrey in person? He looked sort of familiar in the way all old people look vaguely the same to the young. Suddenly, the large, red handkerchief was whisked once more from a jacket pocket and offered to a twitching nose. Bodley lay low until a thunderous triple sneeze had died away.

After that, the old man again began muttering to himself about hay fever, pollen, the desert and so on. Bodley coughed very loudly and wished him good morning. There was no reply. He might have been talking to a brick wall. Becoming bolder, he stepped out from his hiding place between the books and marched up and down the desktop waving his arms. But there was absolutely no reaction from the old man. Suddenly it dawned on him. Not only was he a bear, but an invisible one too, or at least invisible to humans. For Victor Verum had been able to see him, hadn't he?

Invisible or not, instinct told him to find a hiding place. So when he spotted a pouch-like bag made of a colourful textile lying on the desk he crept inside and waited. Before long he dozed off again, and so the morning passed away. It was well past lunch time when the old man gathered together his papers into an untidy bundle and stuffed them into the bag that he slung over his shoulder. He was making ready to leave the library. The sudden movement awoke Bodley.

He quickly realised what was happening. But it was too late to escape. Looking about he spotted the luminous green eyes of Victor Verum, now very much paler in the bright daylight, peering out of an old book.

"Off on your travels already, Bodley?"

Bodley could do no more than wave a paw.

"What a shame you're leaving. We'd only just got acquainted. But if our paths should ever cross again, and I have a curious feeling they will, I would be most pleased to continue our little chat. I do so enjoy hearing the views and opinions of others, don't you?"

"Well, er ..."

"Anyway, I now plan to bite my way right through the Britannica. The whole luscious lot from A to Z. Decidedly daring, don't you think?"

"Well, er ..."

"So it's *arriverdici*, my friend. *Che sara sara*, as they say in *Roma*. I'm simply red hot in *Italiano* by the way. Absolutely *numero uno*."

Bodley remembered that he wanted to ask the bookworm something. But the old man now headed for the door with Bodley trapped in his shoulder bag. So he bade a silent farewell to Victor Verum, poised for action on volume one of the Encyclopaedia Britannica.

As soon as they were outside in the open air, Bodley took in every detail of the scene. The street was filled with a crowd of excited people watching a grand procession of worthy gentlemen all wearing long black gowns with colourful trimmings. Their heads sported tasselled hats and mortarboards. They shuffled slowly past in a cloud of chalk dust. To Bodley, they looked like a herd of headmasters on a school outing.

The old man stood there rooted to the spot, quite absorbed in the proceedings. He looked puzzled, as if trying to figure out something that eluded him. Then an expression of shocked surprise spread across his face as finally the truth revealed itself.

"By the beard of Amenophis! Today is *The Great Midsummer Perambulation of Oxford Professors* and I should be out there marching along with my learned brethren in my best academic robe, not standing here on the pavement like a clueless tourist."

Sadly, he watched his colleagues file past in all their professorial finery. Like pairs of animals boarding Noah's Ark, they disappeared two by two into the great columned entrance of a noble building.

"Oh dear! Where will my absent-mindedness land me? One day I'm sure I shall forget something vitally important. Something simply enormous, and with really serious consequences. Come to think of it, I'm not sure if I haven't done so already. But I can't for the life of me remember what it is."

Shaking his head in self-reproach, he unlocked his rickety old bicycle from an iron railing and placed the bag in a wicker basket attached to the handlebars. From this position Bodley was able to examine the old man as he cycled along.

His wrinkled eyes had a misty, faraway look. He wore a crumpled linen jacket and baggy grey trousers of great antiquity. He sported a battered Panama hat, which might easily have been in use when the Panama Canal was being built. He was shod in cracked leather sandals of a style probably all the rage many centuries ago when the Romans ruled the land.

Bodley's spirits rose at the approach of a group of boys and girls whizzing by on roller blades. He felt an urge to join them. But the children passed quickly by in a colourful blur of movement, laughing and joking among themselves in a happy world of their own. They didn't even notice him.

Journey's end was a tumbledown stone cottage overgrown with roses. Elegant spiders' webs adorned the porch. Thick leaves covered the windows. Sunshine seeped through in golden blobs tinged with green. The old man pushed open the front door and went inside. He dropped the bag onto a threadbare sofa full of squeaking springs. Bodley crawled out and took in the scene. He gazed with amazement at a chaotic jumble of exotic oriental stuff you'd normally expect to find in a museum or an antiques shop. There was no sign of a TV or computer, just a rusty old manual typewriter half buried under a heap of books and documents.

Bodley had never seen so much paper before. A large table had almost disappeared beneath a mountain of letters. He read a couple of the envelopes. They were addressed to Percival Parchment Esq., Professor of Extremely Ancient Archaeology, Amnesia Cottage, Oblivion Avenue, Oxford. So that was where he had landed. But it didn't make any sense at all.

Not knowing what else to do, Bodley sat back and watched the Prof potter about, rummaging here, there and everywhere as if playing his own private version of hide-and-seek. For no sooner had the old man found a book or a scrap of paper and put it down somewhere handy than he would begin frantically to search for it again just about everywhere except the one place he had put it. Then, when he was finally ready to start work he started looking for the spectacles that were sitting on his nose.

"By the beard of Amenophis! If I'm not careful I shall lose my own head next."

Bodley stepped out into the garden to clear his head. A bumpy lawn led down to a narrow channel of water. On the other side, an uncut meadow blew this way and that in the summer breeze. The main river beyond glinted brightly through wild grass speckled with flowers. In the distance, a herd of cows ambled slowly past, cutting a dash in their stylish black and white outfits. He found a shady spot next to a bush and tried to think things through. Could it be he had always been a bear? Somehow it felt natural. But in the drowsy afternoon heat it was impossible to be sure of anything. So perhaps his memory was no better than that of Professor Percival Parchment?

Suddenly, a hush fell. Everything was completely silent. As if the world was holding its breath. Then a tall tree rustled its branches like a huge bird shaking its feathers. Bodley gazed up spellbound at the sky and then down at the water. His mind went curiously numb. All his cares and concerns were carried off unanswered by the stream. Even the thought in progress inside his head petered out in a foggy fuzz of forgetfulness. The strange magic of Amnesia Cottage, Oblivion Avenue, Oxford was already working its spell.

ON THE RIVER

He dozed until the late afternoon sun dropped low in the sky and the dark mirror of the still water in the creek reflected the pink-bellied clouds. Now all was muffled in the hush of evening. Bodley was lost in thought as he strolled about the garden.

He sorely missed the company of the chatty Victor Verum. He felt a tearful twinge and the sad tug of something rather like homesickness. This was rather unsettling since he had no idea where home was. But the sweet sigh of the soft breeze reassured him that things were arranged precisely as they were meant to be, even if everything was unknown and unknowable.

Just as night fell, he spotted two hazy shapes floating on the creek, murky patches of ghostly white in the inky gloom. But they drifted away before he could see what they were. After that, Bodley slumbered on the soft grass until a hooting owl roused him in the wee small hours. Now the full moon was out and he could see two swans floating on the water, their long necks curled back and heads tucked beneath a wing. With one paddle hoisted and the other hanging limply like a loose rudder, the sleeping swans were pushed this way and that by the soft caress of the night breeze on their feathers. He awoke once more just before dawn and looked out for the swans. But they had vanished.

The sun was well up when Bodley was woken by a loud buzzing sound that filled his head. A bewildered bumblebee emerged from his left ear.

"Ever so sorry, dear. Your ear looked just like a hollyhock. At least to me it did. They really should issue us with specs. Belinda's the name by the way."

He didn't care what his ear looked like. He was simply overjoyed someone could actually see him.

"And mine's Bodley. I say, Belinda, I wonder if you could tell me..."

There was something right on the tip of his tongue but he couldn't quite get hold of it. Most of yesterday had been spent looking for answers. Today he couldn't even remember the questions.

"Can't stop now, Bodley. It's all go this morning. Running late as it is. Catch up with you later. Byeee."

The bumblebee flew off towards a tangle of cornflowers. Bodley rubbed the sleepdust from his eyes. He glanced inside the house. No sign of the Prof. He went round to the front door. The bike was missing. Perhaps he had gone back to Duke Humfrey's Library. Not knowing what to do, Bodley sat down and stared vaguely at the swirling eddies of water in the creek. He didn't notice the silent approach of two swans.

"Look, Celia. It's that bear we saw sleeping behind the tree stump last night."

"So it is, Cedric."

They glided up silently behind him.

"I say, good morning, old chap."

Bodley practically jumped out of his bearskin. First a bumblebee and now a swan talking to him. This can't be happening for real.

"You mean you can see me?"

"Yes, of course we can. What a curious question. Why ever not? But I don't think we've seen you around here before, now have we?"

"Well, er ... No, I don't suppose you have."

Suddenly there was no stopping Bodley. His words came thick and fast.

"I saw you two snoozing on the water last night. Pretty cool how you used your backs as pillows. I'd try that myself, but my neck isn't half long enough and it doesn't stretch. In any case I'd sink to the bottom. Each to his own, I guess. With this shaggy coat I can make myself snug just about anywhere. Unless it's damp. Don't think bears like damp. Except for polar bears, I suppose. They sleep on ice. Just imagine that. Don't know how they keep warm. They say you get used to everything. That is, if you have to and ..."

"Excuse me, but are you always so talkative?"

Bodley was surprised to discover that he too was as full of talk as everyone else in this strange place.

"I don't think I used to talk so much before I landed up here. But I'm not really sure."

"Well, I wouldn't worry. Spouting long sentences is just about all they seem to do around here. I think the river is simply there to wash away all the silly old words. Anyway, we are delighted to make your acquaintance. I am Cedric, and this is Celia, my spouse and soul mate. And you are?"

A small voice deep inside him told him it was odd for him to be talking to swans. But who was he to talk? A bear? While he thought about that the swans circled one another, exchanging quizzical glances.

"Does this bear have a name?"

"A name? Yes, of course. Bodley. At least that's what my best chum Victor Verum calls me. *Servitum vostrum* and all that. Speaks half a dozen lingos, you know. I've been staying with him at Duke Humfrey's place. But the real problem is, I don't know who I really am. You see, I'm not sure I have always been a bear. In fact, I'm sure I haven't. But I can't think what else I might have been. Perhaps you can help?"

"I'm not sure we can. We like to keep things simple. We are swans. We look like swans, we act like swans, we talk like swans. When we think, we have swannish thoughts and whenever we can we swan up and down the river. That's quite enough for us. So just be good at being who or what you are. Don't worry about anything else. The rest will look after itself."

Bodley saw there was no point pursuing the *who am I?* question with the swans. They didn't understand there could even be a question.

"So why not join us for a day out on the river? We'll show you what being a swan is all about. Besides, the river is always the best place to sort things out."

The offer was too good to think twice about. Or even once. Cedric had barely opened his wings when

35

Bodley launched himself from the bank across the water. He landed with a heavy thud on the swan's back.

"I say, steady on, old chap."

"Sorry about that, Cedric."

"Just settle down and make yourself comfortable, Bodley, young friend."

"Gosh, it is cosy on board."

"On board? I'm not one of those ghastly tourist excursion boats, you know."

The two swans swam down the creek and out of the smooth waters into the bubbling mainstream of the river. Bodley relaxed on his plush seat of white feathers. It felt like a floating throne, so much finer than that of any king or emperor.

Cedric's powerful paddles ensured steady progress downstream. Celia followed close behind.

"I say, isn't this simply wonderful and just the very best way to see the world?"

"No need to shout, Bodley. The river is a place for calm reflection."

He now addressed Celia in a quieter voice.

"Do you often come to the Prof's garden?"

"We always build our nest there. Each and every year without fail. Amnesia Cottage is such a lovely spot. Very private too. Professor Parchment takes care we are not disturbed."

"Do you have any ... er?"

"You mean cygnets?"

Bodley nodded.

"Well, to be perfectly honest, we have so many we are almost running out of sibilants."

"Sibilants?"

"Yes, sibilants. Swans must all have names that begin with an *S* sound: Sara, Simon, Samantha, Cylla, Sid, Sebastian, Sibyl, and so on. It's becoming harder and harder to find ones we haven't used before."

"How about Cyril?"

Cedric slowly shook his graceful neck at Bodley's helpful suggestion.

"I'm afraid that's one name we can't possibly use. Every last squirrel calls itself Cyril. You can understand why of course. Though that makes Cyril a complete non-starter for us swans."

"But surely if every squirrel is called Cyril, it must be very confusing for them. How on earth do they know who they are talking about?"

Cedric thought a while on this.

"An excellent question. I really don't know the answer. But it doesn't seem to bother them. When one Cyril refers to another Cyril all the squirrels seem to know immediately which particular Cyril is meant. So perhaps squirrels are smarter than they look."

After this the conversation flagged a bit, so Celia introduced a change of subject.

"I must say, Bodley. You do look rather young to be gadding about on your own. I trust your parents know where you are?"

That reminded him of his question.

"Well, that's a bit of a problem actually. I was wondering if perhaps you…"

The mooing of two exceedingly large cows interrupted Bodley.

"Lord love a duck! Take a look at that, Gertie."

"Well I never, Daisy."

"A bear on a swan's back, if you don't mind."

"They're coming this way."

"It's a free country, I suppose."

"No thought for the privacy of others having a spot of lunch though, is there?"

"Folk seem to think they can treat the open river as a public highway."

"Forget it runs right through our front parlour."

"Looks very pleased with himself that bear."

"Just like our fat farmer sprawled out in his big comfy armchair."

"Well, they're off now."

"Good riddance, I say."

"Can't see much sense in swans myself."

"Nor bears neither."

"Munching grass and pumping milk is what I'd call a proper job, Gertie."

"And a full udder at the end of the day, Daisy."

"That's right, my dear. Something useful to show for your efforts."

The conversation faded away, leaving Bodley with grave doubts about what sort of place Oxford was, where even the cows talked about the oddest things.

Meanwhile, Cedric and Celia paddled on slowly downstream. They glided serenely past a pride of professors basking in the long grass, stark naked but for floppy cotton hats to keep their brains cool. A buzz of brilliant ideas arose from this meadow full of learned men as if from a nest of hornets.

The swans sailed on serenely under a high round bridge from which young boys hurled themselves with blood-curdling screams into the water. Bodley thought it looked like jolly good fun. Cedric remarked you would never catch a swan doing anything so foolish. As Bodley looked down, he glimpsed his own reflection in the water. He really was a bear, and no mistake.

At that very moment Cedric veered sharply to avoid a floating log. Bodley wobbled, tottered, and wobbled again, finally falling head over heels into the river. Down he went, then up he came, kicking and spluttering for all he was worth. To his surprise, he found he was swimming. He didn't know he could. But it was Celia's graceful neck supporting him. For a while the swan kindly let him enjoy the wonderful sensation of floating free in the refreshingly cool water. Bodley instantly felt lighter, as if all his cares were drifting gently away with the silent current. Nothing seemed to matter quite so much any more.

Celia helped him scramble onto Cedric's back.

"I reckon that little dip in the river has made you one of us, Bodley."

Bodley reckoned he hadn't been a bear all that long. Was he now turning into a swan?

Celia read his thoughts.

"Don't worry, Bodley. You aren't going to sprout feathers or anything."

The swans now took him on a tour of all their favourite places along the riverbank. They showed him mysterious backwaters lined with poplars where no one could see them but the crows in their lofty nests. They passed behind the trailing branches of weeping willows to peep out through a curtain of greenery at a convoy of coots floating downstream. Then they basked in the sun by a field of golden corn fringed with red poppies. The bear's soggy fur soon dried out in the heat.

They paddled on until they came to a vast meadow where scores of horses roamed free as wild antelope on the plains of Africa. For lunch, Cedric and Celia fished up some slimy weed from the riverbed. It didn't look all that tasty so Bodley ate two juicy apples from a tree instead. They whiled away the long, hot afternoon in idle pursuits. Bodley enjoyed another dip, this time without swallowing half the river. It seemed to him this was the loveliest place on earth. At last they headed for home. It was almost dark when they entered the creek by Parchment's garden.

"We'll be paddling all the way upstream in a day or so. As far as the river goes. We always do the trip in high summer. To pay respects to Old Father Thames. Possibly he's the one to help you with all those questions of yours. He has an answer for everything. We'll drop by for you when we're ready to set off."

Bodley thanked them, wished them good night and stumbled sleepily over the lawn to a tree stump not far from the water's edge. He was just about ready to drop, when a stern challenge halted him in his tracks.

"Stop! Who goes there?"

He looked up to see a solitary bumblebee on a small ledge by a hole in the tree stump.

"I said, stop! Who goes there? Stop, or I'll ..."

Bodley stepped out of the dark shadow into the bright moonlight.

"Good night, Belinda. It's only me, Bodley."

"It's *only* you, is it? You do realise they could court-martial me for fraternising with the enemy?"

"The enemy?"

"Yes, the enemy. What do you think? Bears are public enemy number one. Always after our honey. I've been trained to sting on sight. According to the rules, I should be sounding the alarm."

"Steady on, Belinda. I may look like a bear. But I don't go around stealing honey."

"Maybe not. I only have your word for it."

"What I mean is that this particular bear won't be raiding your hive for honey or anything like that."

"We're not a hive, as it happens. Hives are for the honeybees. We humble bumbles live in the wild. Our colony nests in a crevice beneath this tree stump. Oh dear, I shouldn't have told you that! That's meant to be top secret. Now I'll really be in for it."

"Don't worry, Belinda. I won't tell anyone, not a soul. Honest, I won't."

"You mustn't. Promise you won't. You've no idea what a tough lot the drones are. Always giving us a hard time, and they just laze about while we working women are at it non-stop, flying here, there and everywhere until our wings are fit to drop. Sheer exploitation, if you ask me. Did you know some crazy professor has proved it's impossible for us even to take off, let alone fly with a full load of pollen? But just you try telling the drones that."

Bodley yawned. Why did everyone in Oxford have so much to say about everything under the sun? That was his very last thought of the day before he fell asleep. Belinda realised there was nothing for it but to let sleeping bears lie. First thing in the morning she would give him a buzz in the ear and move him on.

B odley was woken very early by an urgent buzz in the ear. Belinda was extremely anxious to see him move away from the colony.

"Wakey, wakey! Rise and shine, you snoozehead. Time to be finding somewhere else to sleep."

With that Belinda flew off. When Bodley opened his eyes the bumblebee was nowhere to be seen. Finding no-one in the garden, he entered the house where Professor Parchment was already busy at his desk, scratching away with a spluttering fountain pen, totally absorbed in what he was doing. Gradually, a broad smile spread slowly across the old man's face and he permitted himself a chuckle of satisfaction.

"By the beard of Amenophis! Finished at last."

Professor Parchment hummed contentedly as he gathered up the scattered pages into an untidy bundle that he wrapped in brown paper and tied up with string. He inscribed two large capital letters MS to remind himself what was inside, then patted the parcel fondly as if it were the head of a much-loved grandchild.

"A lost world saved, and it's all in here. Just a few references to check, then it's ready to go off to the publisher. I'll get cracking straight away."

All this sounded very mysterious to Bodley who wondered how something as large as a lost world could possibly fit into so small a packet.

Suddenly, Belinda flew in through the window.

"I reckon the Prof's off to London today. I'd tag along, if I were you."

"London?"

"London, you don't know London? It's the big city. Mother of them all. You'll love it or hate it. But you simply must see it. At least, that's what they say."

"Haven't you been to London, Belinda?"

"You must be joking. We workers don't get to go anywhere. The drones never give us a day off. Must dash now. If I were you I'd hide in the Prof's bag. He takes it with him everywhere. See you later. Byeee."

So why not tag along and go to London? Bodley climbed onto the sofa, hid in the bag that had carried him out of the Bodleian Library and waited. Professor Parchment soon picked it up. But once outside, he stopped, scratched his head, hung the bag on a branch of a tree and went back indoors.

Bodley stuck out his head to find himself dangling high above the ground. At that very moment, Belinda flew past on some errand in that curious zigzag fashion so popular with bumblebees.

"I say, Belinda! Come here a moment!"

"Who's that? Oh, it's you. What's going on? I thought you were off to London."

"So did I. But the Prof has left me dangling up here. Can't say I like it very much."

"Don't worry. I expect he has gone back for something. Quite absent-minded is our Professor Parchment. But I'm sure he won't leave you behind."

Belinda had other things on her mind.

"Haven't seen your flashy pal this morning, have you? Cute little fellow. Gorgeous, green eyes. Really big. Probably magnified by his specs though."

"Victor?"

"That's the one."

"Victor Verum is here?"

"*Was* here, more like it. We had quite a long chat yesterday evening. Funny way of talking he has, our Victor. *Servitum vostrum* and all that. Ever so posh."

"But Belinda ..."

"Quite full of himself he was. Bit of a show off, actually. What he didn't know wasn't worth knowing."

"But Belinda, why didn't you tell me Victor was here? I must see him. Something I simply must ask him. It's urgent. Really urgent."

"He wants to see you too. Asked me to give you his *complimenti*. His *complimenti*, if you please. Yes, I think that was it. Now isn't that lovely?"

"If I had only known Victor was here, I ..."

"But there's neither sight nor sound of him this morning. Didn't strike me as the type to do a runner. But you never can tell with blokes, can you?"

"Look, Belinda. You've just got to help me down from here. Then we'll go and look for Victor. I must speak to him. Simply must, or I'll ..."

Professor Parchment now re-appeared, clutching his brown paper parcel.

"Silly old me. I only forgot the most important thing. Whatever next?"

Belinda smiled as she shook her head.

"Don't look so glum. You'll have a grand time in London. Just stick with the Prof and you'll come back safe and sound. Now I really must dash. Byeee."

Bodley watched sadly as Belinda flew off. To add to his unhappiness, he now saw Cedric and Celia come sailing into the creek. Their graceful necks arched enquiringly as they scanned the garden. Were they looking for him? Perhaps take him along on their trip upstream to visit Old Father Thames? That would have been just perfect. There was nothing Bodley would have liked better than to be out on the river with the two swans. That was where he wanted to be. He ached desperately at being parted from his new friends.

By contrast, Professor Parchment was in high spirits. He whistled merrily as he took the bag down from the tree and slipped in the brown paper package. Bodley moved over sharply to make space for it.

Next thing he knew he was in the wicker basket of the bike and heading into town. By the time he thought it safe to peep out, he was on board a bus racing along a motorway set in a deep cutting gouged out of the hillside. He glanced back at the fields and villages behind. Then he turned to face the great big unknown rushing toward him at high speed. He had a bad feeling about London. But it was too late now.

LOST AND FOUND

London came into view first as a dirty smudge on the horizon. Then it gradually took shape as a dense mass of tall buildings standing shoulder to shoulder. The bus swooped up onto an overpass, then whizzed along for several minutes at rooftop level and finally got stuck in a solid jam of traffic. Ages later, the driver announced they had reached Marble Arch.

They got off and caught a number 7 red double-decker. It shunted painfully along Oxford Street at a snail's pace. At last, it shuddered to a halt by a huge building with soaring columns. Professor Parchment entered a tall iron gate, crossed a wide forecourt and made for a broad flight of stone steps.

A couple of fat pigeons appeared to be in charge. They waddled about importantly like sergeant majors, passing comment on all and sundry.

"Mis'rable looking lot this morning, Fred."

"As per usual, Joe."

"Par for the course, I'd say."

Bodley didn't like the look of these two grumpy overweight pigeons.

"'Ere, take a butchers at that bear in the old geezer's bag."

"All right for some, innit?"

"Flamin' cheek."

"Riding about like flippin' royalty."

Bodley ducked out of sight. But the two pigeons continued to taunt him.

"Oi! Where d'you fink you're goin', mate?"

"They don't let no blinkin' bears in the BM!"

The BM? Then he spotted a sign. The British Museum. So that's where the Prof was heading. Bodley remained hidden until safely inside, well away from the taunting remarks of the two pigeons. When he peeped out of the bag he found himself in a vast circular chamber. A majestic dome arched high above his head. Bookshelves arose on all sides to a great height. Rows of desks radiated like the spokes of a wheel. The professor deposited his bag on one of these and wandered off. Seconds later he scuttled back to retrieve his precious manuscript, which he now clutched protectively to his chest as if it were a small child.

Bodley crawled out of the bag. Hesitantly at first, he strolled along the desktop right under the noses of scholars and researchers. They didn't bat an eyelid. It was as if he didn't exist. So he was completely invisible to all humans just as he was to Professor Parchment.

Well, if he couldn't be seen then why not have some fun with his invisibility? With a great leap he launched himself into space and landed on a passing book barrow pushed along by an aged librarian. Bodley enjoyed the ride as the barrow was pushed here, there and everywhere delivering books. He did the grand tour of the Round Reading Room.

When he had had enough he jumped off and landed on a desk that looked just like his starting point.

But it wasn't. The fun was suddenly over as he realised he didn't know how to get back.

Why had he wandered off on his own? Just stick with the Prof, Belinda had said, and all would be well. Then his heart sank, as far away, he saw Professor Parchment, bag slung over his shoulder, on his way out. He was going to be left behind.

Cold panic gripped him as he realised his folly. Bodley jumped up and down desperately waving his arms. Now his invisibility to humans was no longer such fun. He tried shouting. That was just as useless. His voice couldn't be heard. In fact, there was nothing he could do to draw attention to himself.

A thick lump of despair stuck in his throat as the professor disappeared through a small door under a large clock. Bodley felt utterly lost and abandoned. He feared he would never again find his way back to that idyllic cottage by the river in Oxford. Never again would he awake to the dear buzz of Belinda in his ear or enjoy another ride on a swan's back. He even longed for the caustic comments of Daisy and Gertie, and he would have given anything at that moment simply to hear the soothing voice of Victor Verum.

The day wore on. The afternoon dragged its heels. Finally closing time arrived. He watched with growing numbness of heart as the big round room emptied of its occupants. Now he was completely on his own. He walked about aimlessly, this way and that. He had all the freedom to do whatever he liked. But there seemed no point in anything. He lay down on an ink blotter, weak with misery. Tears could be held back no longer. The floodgates gave way and opened wide. He hated himself for being so weak but it was out of his control. He cried until he was thoroughly exhausted.

At last, sleep released him from his torment. But not for long. He soon awoke in the mellow afterglow of the long summer evening. But this did nothing to brighten his mood. How he wished he hadn't come to London, and that he hadn't gone off on his own. He felt the tears bubble up again. Now they flowed like a swollen stream that had burst its banks. He shut his eyelids in a forlorn attempt to contain them.

Then suddenly, he heard a strange voice.

"Tut tut. Now what do we have here, I wonder? That is no way for a young bear to behave. Not exactly ursine, I must say."

The mystery voice had a pleasant ring to it.

"So, young fuzzy ears. Pray tell me the precise cause and origin of all this fuss and botheration. There is nothing, absolutely nothing, I can assure you, that a spot of cool, concentrated cogitation can't cure."

Bodley stopped breathing. He kept very quiet and refused to lift even a corner of an eyelid, while the mystery voice continued to speak.

"Making such a fuss is not at all ursine, in my learned opinion. Now be a good fellow, turn off the waterworks and pray tell me what this great commotion is all about."

The kindly edge to the voice encouraged Bodley to speak, although still with eyelids closed tight as manhole covers.

"What's ursine supposed to mean?"

"Aha, a sign of intelligent life, methinks. Ursine denotes none other than the species of *ursus*[2] to which you and I have the proud privilege to belong."

---

[2] *Ursus*, Latin for bear.

URSINE ENCOUNTER

Bodley's eyes popped open to behold a dark brown bear of portly girth and mature years, as could be judged from a greying around the muzzle. He wore a green jacket, yellow waistcoat, grey trousers. A pair of half-moon spectacles gave him a scholarly air. He looked studiously at Bodley over their gold rims, as if examining a scientific specimen of considerable interest.

"*Ursus?*"

"Yes, *ursus.*"

"What's that?"

"That's *ursus*, as in Latin for a bear. You're one of us. What else do you think I mean?"

Bodley scrambled to his feet and threw his arms around this stranger come to rescue him in his hour of need. The older bear gave him a generous hug in return and looked down into his upturned face.

"That's better. I think we have had enough of tears and sobs and suchlike and so forth and so on, et cetera. But first things first. I am Bloomsbury. That is Bloomsbury, as in Bloomsbury, which is my nice neck of the woods, my happy hunting ground. In short, and not wanting to overstate the matter, it's my personal patch of paradise, my very own half-acre of heaven."

Bodley, taken aback by this amazing flood of wordage, felt a strange urge to respond in similar style, or at least as best he could.

"Bloomsbury, dear Bloomsbury. I must tell you how pleased, delighted, happy, glad and generally over the moon I am to make your acquaintance. I was so miserable just a moment ago. But now I feel as cheerful and chirpy as a ... as a chimpanzee!"

"Chirpy as a chimpanzee? I'm not sure that one will catch on. Anyway, not bad for starters. But do tell me your name, young fellow."

"My name? It's Bodley. That's Bodley, as in the Bodleian Library. *Servitum vostrum* and suchlike and so forth and so on, et cetera."

"*Servitum vostrum*, Bodleian Library? How super, how splendid, how simply spiffing, my dear Bodley. I see we shall have plenty of mutual interests on which to discuss and deliberate, to pronounce and pontificate in the years ahead."

"Well, I wasn't exactly planning on staying that long, Bloomsbury, and I don't think I would be much good at ... er ... pontifying."

"You mean pontificating, Bodley. The noble art of holding forth on any old subject you care to choose for hours on end regardless of whether anyone is listening or not. There's nothing quite like it."

Bodley looked doubtful.

"Don't worry, I'll show you how it's done. But first, do tell me all about yourself. The full story."

Bloomsbury leaned back comfortably on a thick volume of the Oxford English Dictionary. Bodley took a deep breath and came straight out with his most pressing problem of not knowing who he was, or how he had landed up where he had.

"You see, it's like this. I don't think I've always been a bear."

"You don't think you've always been a bear? Stuff and nonsense! Let me tell you young fellow that bears are born, not made. Therefore it stands to reason that you have always been a bear, and always will be a bear. Nothing else is possible. At the most you are a bear with an identity problem, and that's really quite unheard of too. Since bears are solid creatures, with all four paws firmly on the ground. Perhaps you are a tad confused by your new surroundings. Rest assured, I shall make allowances. Anyway, I suggest we put all that to one side. Just tell me the rest."

So Bodley told the story of the past few days. Bloomsbury made him go over in the greatest detail everything related to the Bodleian Library, while showing very little, in fact no interest at all in his glorious trip on the river with Cedric and Celia. As for Victor Verum, at the very mention of a bespectacled bookworm, Bloomsbury said gruffly that he had heard quite enough about him, even if he could speak half a dozen foreign languages quite fluently, as Bodley assured him that he could. Bloomsbury couldn't imagine anything more awful than a creature that ate books, and no, he didn't even want to know about a bumblebee called Belinda, thank you very much.

"Strange company you've been keeping, Bodley. Anyway, let's skip the talking animals. I'm a bit too old for that sort of thing. Tell me more about your Professor Parchment. You don't mean the very learned Professor Percival Parchment?"

Bodley remembered the name on the envelope.

"Yes, that's the one."

"My, oh my! Most amazing! Staying with the renowned Professor Percival Parchment!"

Bodley shrugged his furry shoulders. He couldn't understand what all the fuss was about.

"Don't tell me you don't know about Professor Parchment. He is the brainiest scholar of his generation. Always coming up with something new to startle the world. An excellent mind. At least, not bad for a mere non-ursine. What he doesn't know about ancient archaeology isn't worth knowing. Now what particular field is he ploughing right now?"

"What particular field, Bloomsbury? Well, the Prof doesn't have an actual field as far as I can tell. But he does have the loveliest garden by the river you can possibly imagine. If you are interested in fields, then you'll have to ask Daisy and Gertie. They live in a huge field full of clover. I'm sure you'd like them. They...."

"What on earth are you talking about, Bodley? More talking animals, I suppose? You make about as much sense as a stuffed bear. I don't mean a field of grass, of corn or clover, but the professor's field of research, his special subject, his current project. In short, what is he working on?"

"Well, I'm not really sure. But he was always scribbling away. He had simply masses of old papers heaped up in huge piles all over the place. Oh yes, and then he tied some of them together in a brown paper parcel, and he wrote something on the paper. Two great big capital letters."

"Letters? What letters? Try to remember."

"Let me see now. Yes, I remember. A capital M and an S. Yes, that was it. MS."

"MS? MS! A manuscript, how exciting!"

Bloomsbury was intrigued to know more.

"So what was in this manuscript?"

"I've no idea."

"But you must have seen something that would give me a clue. For example, what sort of books were on his desk?"

Bodley looked about him.

"Oh, big ones mostly. Quite thick, and rather dusty too. Pretty much like in here. Only maybe not quite so many."

Bloomsbury's gaze now swept around the great circle of bookshelves that towered above them. Bodley followed the movement of his deep, wise eyes. In them were reflected the lofty dome and its precious volumes that were Bloomsbury's pride and joy as if he had written them all himself.

"Most impressive, eh? Everything you'll ever need to know is right under this very roof. There is nowhere else quite like here: the Round Reading Room of the British Museum."

To Bodley, it looked ten times bigger and thus ten times worse than the Bodleian Library.

"But there's nowhere to play, Bloomsbury. No river with swans at the bottom of the garden. In fact, no garden at all. It must get very boring with books wherever you look. Books from wall to wall and from floor to ceiling. Nothing but books, books and ... er ... more books."

Bodley realised that he had gone far too far. Bloomsbury's furry brow wrinkled into a dark, menacing frown, a thunderstorm about to burst.

"Books boring? That is no way for a clueless cub to be talking. If we didn't have books, then where would we put all the words? And what would we do without words? We wouldn't be able to think at all!"

Bodley didn't quite follow the logic of this. But he nodded as if to say he understood perfectly well. As for Bloomsbury, he now seemed for once strangely lost for words. Long moments passed in brooding silence.

"I'm terribly sorry, Bloomsbury. I didn't mean to say all books were boring. Story books are brilliant. The ones with wizards are simply terrific."

Bloomsbury's response to this was immediate and rather puzzling.

"Wizards terrific? You want to know what I say to wizards? Well, I say blizzards to wizards! Too much gas in their gizzards!"

Bloomsbury looked incandescent, as if he was about to explode.

"Who needs wizards and their mumbo-jumbo? At any rate, we bears certainly don't. I'll tell you why one day when you are a little bit older."

That day arrived much sooner than Bodley expected. For Bloomsbury now fixed him with a steely look as he began to explain.

"We bears are wizards too in our own way. We have a special gift for making magic with words. The trick is to learn as many words as you can, especially the long, difficult ones no one can pronounce. Then, if you string enough of them together, and in the right order of course, then hey presto!"

Bloomsbury paused for dramatic effect. Bodley noted that his eyes had the same misty, faraway gaze as Professor Parchment's.

"Hey presto! You have made something out of nothing. If that isn't magic, then I don't know what is. Words will get you to the moon and back. With words you can seize the secret of the universe and hold it in your paw. Now doesn't that beat a few silly spells?"

Bodley didn't know what to say. So he decided to say nothing at all and let Bloomsbury proceed to the end of his lecture.

"So, in conclusion, dear Bodley, pray take careful note and be officially advised that it is our very special ursine gift to be regular wizards with words. It is what we bears are best at, and if we reach the summit of our ambitions and think the Big Idea itself, then there's a special treat in store."

Bloomsbury looked around to make sure they were quite alone.

"Then we get to meet a bear in a million, one way above all others. In fact, so far above us we can't even see him."

He now continued in hushed tones.

"I mean the Great Bear, no less. The Great Bear knows absolutely everything there is to know about absolutely everything there is to know about. They say he lives somewhere up there among the bright stars in the night sky. Can you imagine anything more exciting than that, young Bodley?"

Bodley gazed up into the great dome. Through the skylight he saw night had fallen and the stars were twinkling. But Bloomsbury was not to be stopped.

"Where, you might ask, is all this leading? Well, since you didn't ask, I am not strictly bound to say. However, and this is just between ourselves, let me tell you that very soon I aim to take my place at the feet of the Great Bear. I have it almost within my grasp. But the last bit is taking longer than I ever thought possible. So what I really need right now is a research assistant to speed things up. As it happens, the post is vacant. So what do you say?"

"Well, I'm jolly glad you told me all that, but..."

"Excellent. The job is yours, Bodley. Consider yourself appointed. You can begin at once."

"But I must be getting back. My parents will be wondering if ..."

"Yes? If what?"

"Oh nothing. It's just that I'm not really sure if I have any ..."

"Any what?"

"Well, parents, actually."

"How very curious. Well, you must have parents somewhere, especially since you have just mentioned them."

Bloomsbury scratched his head.

"On the other hand, if you really don't have any parents, then I suggest that..."

A long pause ensued. Something melted in a long-forgotten, tender place deep inside the old bear at a hazy memory of being bounced on the knees of a loving Ma and Pa Bloomsbury. When he spoke again, his tone had softened.

"You mustn't worry, dear Bodley. Things will sort themselves out. Your parents will turn up, I'm sure. Perhaps they've mislaid you. So don't look so glum. Meanwhile, you can stay with me. Anyway, I expect you are wondering what's for supper?"

"Well, I did miss out on lunch today."

"So be my guest. I insist. The British Museum dining facilities are quite adequate. In fact, the menu is far from boring."

Things were looking up. Fortune couldn't have sent him a better companion. Already he felt so close, they might almost be related. It was all quite uncanny: strange but yet familiar at the same time. Perhaps he had always been a bear and somehow managed to forget all about it? At any rate, Bloomsbury's absolute certainty on that score permitted no doubt. His utter ursine authority was indeed most reassuring.

Bloomsbury slid onto a chair and down to the ground. Bodley followed. The two bears emerged from the Round Reading Room into the foyer of the British Museum. A huge staircase wide as a street soared up to their right. They proceeded instead past a bookshop. More books, thought Bodley. There is no end to them. Heaven knows how many words they must contain. Would he have to learn them all by heart? Inwardly, he groaned at the prospect. But this time he kept his thoughts to himself.

"I'm so glad you found me, Bloomsbury. Humans just seem to look right through you as if you weren't there at all. They don't even see you."

He was about to add that at least talking animals could see you and have quite a bit to say for themselves but he thought better of it.

"Yes, Bodley. Distinctly odd, isn't it? Can't say I bother much with humans. Unless of course they've been turned into statues."

"Turned into statues?"

"Yes, seems to knock some sense into them, once they've been turned into figures of marble, granite or bronze. Some of my best friends are statues. Tell you what. I'll introduce you to some after dinner."

They reached the restaurant. Bloomsbury strode boldly into the kitchen and made straight for the fridge. He swung open the door with a flourish as if about to enter a banqueting hall. The two bears were greeted by the sight of shelves laden with food and drink.

"Just feast your eyes on that, Bodley. Then fill that empty tummy of yours. Our meeting is a cause for celebration. So we shall eat and drink as much as we can. Or perhaps just a tiny bit more."

STRANGERS IN THE NIGHT

No sooner had Bodley restored his belly to its normal state of fleshy roundness than he felt incredibly drowsy. First a couple of small yawns, then a monstrous third yawn forced his jaws wide open.

"I say, Bloomsbury, you must excuse me. That was a delicious dinner, a marvellous meal, a ..."

Bodley yawned again. So Bloomsbury finished off his sentence for him.

"... a superb supper, a fabulous feast, a royal repast, a splendid spread, a bountiful banquet and so on and suchlike and so forth et cetera. I know it's late and you are tired. But it's high time you met some of my statuesque friends in here. Members of my extended family, you might say."

Bloomsbury took Bodley firmly by the paw and led him into a gallery full of the strangest sculptures. They halted by two identical statues. Each had the body of a monumental lion with curved wings crowned by the head and shoulders of a bearded warrior. Their harsh, impassive faces stared straight ahead, like an enormous pair of grotesque bookends.

"The Winged Lions of Nimrud, Bodley. They may look frightening, but they're supposed too. That's their job. They guard the city against subversive enemy agents. Underneath they are pretty decent chaps. Though they don't like to admit it."

Bloomsbury whispered something and waited. Nothing happened. Then, all of a sudden, the Winged Lions of Nimrud came to life.

"In the name of mighty Ashurnasirpal, who goes there?"

The two statues spoke with one voice.

"Who wishes to enter the noble city of Nimrud?"

"Salutations, great guardians of Nimrud. It is I, Bloomsbury. All respect to mighty Ashurnasirpal. Also from my young friend Bodley. He's new here."

Bodley stepped forward hesitantly.

"Pleased to meet you. *Servitum vostrum*."

"Welcome to Nimrud. Seat of all power. Source of all knowledge."

Bodley repeated the phrase.

"Source of all knowledge?"

"Do you dare to doubt our powers?"

"Well, er ... No, of course not."

"If you don't believe us, then you must test us. That's the rules. So ask whatever you like. All questions answered. Nothing too difficult."

This was a formal command not an invitation. But Bodley couldn't think of anything to ask except for the one big question on his mind. Who was he? He didn't really want to ask it, at least not after Bloomsbury's categorical reassurance that he really was exactly what he looked like, namely a bear. But he couldn't do anything to stop the question. It simply popped out of its own accord.

"Who am I?"

This took both the Winged Lions of Nimrud completely by surprise. Not the sort of thing they had ever been asked before. Their magnificent curled beards quivered as their jaws dropped. But not a sound issued from their mouths.

"Yes, who am I? Perhaps it's not really that important, but I seem to have forgotten who I am. So that's my question. Who am I?"

The Winged Lions of Nimrud looked perplexed, even a shade angry.

"Who am I? What sort of a question is that? Most singular. Doesn't make any sense. Who are *we*? Now, that is a proper question. So we'll answer that one. *We* are the Winged Lions of Nimrud! That's who *we* are. Next question!"

"But that's cheating."

Bodley's sense of fair play got the better of him. Now he surprised even himself by his own daring.

"But that's not what I asked. Who am 'I'? That is the question."

The two Winged Lions of Nimrud exchanged worried looks. They were not used to being challenged in this bold manner by a young bear, and such a pushy little fellow at that. For now he had found his voice, Bodley was in no mood to let them off the hook that easily. He approached each Winged Lion in turn and repeated the *Who am I?* question. The Winged Lions of Nimrud could only repeat it over and over, like a record stuck in the groove.

This was going nowhere. Bloomsbury whispered in Bodley's ear.

"Oh dear, perhaps that wasn't such a good idea, Bodley. You have to ask them something they already know. That's how it's done. Or else they get unhappy. Besides, since they can only think of themselves as a pair, everything must come in twos. They can't cope with ones."

Bloomsbury steered Bodley away.

"We'd better go now. Before they get even more confused. I do hope they manage to sort themselves out."

They were hardly out of earshot of the Winged Lions of Nimrud when they arrived at the huge head of an Egyptian pharaoh mounted on a lofty plinth.

Bloomsbury spoke in a whisper.

"This is Amenophis III. Pharaoh of all Egypt, ruler of the Nile around three thousand three hundred and thirty three years ago. He has been around a tiny bit longer than the Winged Lions of Nimrud."

Amenophis? Bodley now recalled how Professor Parchment had mentioned the beard of Amenophis several times. But where was it? Poor old Amenophis appeared to have lost not only his entire beard but a great big chunk of his chin as well. To make matters worse, a fragment of his mutilated arm lay on the ground by his side. But in spite of all this damage, the majestic expression on the Pharaoh's face still commanded fear and respect.

Bloomsbury now began to speak in a resounding voice full of pomp and circumstance.

"Greetings, oh Mighty One, Lord of the Nile, Father of the Planet, Creator of the World, Master of the Universe, Cosmic Ruler, Supreme Being."

Slowly, the lips of the Pharaoh began to move.

"Yes, yes, yes. That will do. Spare me the rest. I've heard it so many times before. What a crashing bore it is, when everyone cringes and tells the most shameless fibs about one's Pharaonic magnificence."

Amenophis III now noticed Bodley.

"You are new around here. Who are you?"

Bloomsbury quickly made the introductions.

"This is Bodley, my new research assistant, just down from Oxford. He has been staying with Professor Parchment."

Amenophis III showed a tiny flicker of interest.

"Parchment, eh? The old fellow really should call himself Papyrus, don't you reckon? Since he is so very interested in ancient Egypt."

Amenophis III paused briefly for Bloomsbury to chuckle politely at his witty remark.

"So when is Parchment going to finish that book of his? He's been working on it long enough. I trust he'll have some nice things to say about me. Rather hoping I'll be on the cover, actually. Not like this of course. But how I used to be. When I was in my prime. All parts intact and joined together."

The full weight of Amenophis III's attention now returned to Bodley.

"What did you say your name was, small furry, insignificant creature?"

"Well, Bodley is the name I'm using. But I don't really know if it's mine. To tell the truth, I've forgotten who I am, you see."

Oh dear, thought Bloomsbury. Here we go again. But he couldn't risk interrupting and changing the subject while Amenophis III was speaking.

"Forgotten who you are? Lost your label, have you? Now, if you lived in here you would have a neat little sign on you with your name printed on it. So it wouldn't matter if you forgot who you are from time to time. By the way, I trust you're not planning to become an exhibit, are you? It's not as easy as it looks, you know. Standing still all day is only the half of it. You have to have been someone. Someone very special. They don't take just anyone in the British Museum, and certainly not small, hairy animals. Unless you've been mummified, of course. Now I'm getting bored. So that is all I shall tell you."

Just when Bloomsbury was breathing a sigh of relief that the conversation hadn't gone too badly, Bodley rashly decided to ask his question.

"But there is one more thing which I'm sure you can tell me."

"Tell you what?"

"Who am I? You see I'm trying to find out who I am. I'm sure you can help. You must know everything, absolutely everything."

Amenophis III smiled in a superior kind of way.

"Well, yes, naturally. As it happens, I do know absolutely everything. Of course I do."

This prompted a sudden outburst of female giggling from the shadows behind the Pharaoh. Bodley could just make out four figures of black granite, two seated, two standing: slinky, long-legged and small-breasted just like fashion models. Only they had the heads of lionesses. Now all four of them began to talk, one after the other, in a rasping, purring sort of patter.

"Silly old Amenophis. All granite between the ears. Better ask us. The simply sizzling Sakhmet Sisters[3]. Egypt's greatest girl group in the 18th Dynasty. Top of the charts on both banks of the Nile. Like to hear our latest single?"

Amenophis III indicated with an upward roll of his eyes that he was all too accustomed to the merciless teasing of the Sakhmet Sisters.

"Latest single? Who are they trying to kid? Their newest release must be older than the Sphinx."

Amenophis III now addressed himself directly to the Sakhmet Sisters who were giggling out of control like silly schoolgirls.

"All right, girls. Calm down. You've had your little joke. Just don't forget who made you famous in the first place."

Amenophis III turned again to the two bears.

---

[3] The goddess Sakhmet was adored by Amenophis III who had many statues made in her honour.

"Falling for the Sakhmet Sisters must be the daftest thing I ever did. I bought all their albums. Plastered their posters all over the palace. Even had one stuck on my tomb. Without me, they would have gone nowhere. What thanks do I get? Now they poke fun at me behind my back. "

Amenophis III sighed.

"Where is the justice in that? Besides, four against one isn't fair."

The Sakhmet Sisters now broke into what sounded like a football chant.

"Four One. Four One. Four One. Four One."

"See what I mean. It's hopeless. Quite hopeless."

This only prompted a fresh outburst of girlish giggling from the Sakhmet Sisters. The Pharaoh continued in a soft whisper.

"I'm still their number one fan actually. Don't know why. Can't help myself. But don't tell them I said so. In fact, I'm their only fan. That must be why they find me so frightfully amusing."

Now Amenophis III spoke directly to Bodley.

"So, what was it you wanted to know, small insignificant furry creature?"

"Well, actually..."

Bodley hesitated.

"Actually, what? Speak!"

A Pharaoh had to be obeyed. So dutifully Bodley obliged by revealing his question.

"Who am I? That's all."

"Who am I? That's all, is it? Who am I? Wouldn't we all like to know the answer to that? When I ran the show, anyone who dared ask such an insolent question had to carve a hundred thousand hieroglyphs: I am no one. I am no one. I am no one."

Amenophis III stared at Bodley like the sternest of stern of headmasters.

"So who am I? They called me Amenophis III. Three, if you please. How would you like a number for a surname? Makes me sound like a sequel to some daft Hollywood movie. Hardly the thing for a Pharaoh."

Amenophis III took a deep breath.

"Well, who am I then? Take a good look, young fellow. I once commanded the mightiest empire in the world. I held the keys of life and death for my terrified subjects. But who am I now? All I am is what you see. My smashed arm lies before me like a broken branch. The other parts of my body are buried in the sands at Karnak. Dashed inconvenient, having one's head and forearm in London and the rest of one's Pharaonic person in Egypt. Who am I indeed? I don't even know where I am. Perhaps you can tell me?"

Now Bodley noticed the left ear of Amenophis III was also missing. He reckoned there must indeed be more of him in Egypt than in London.

But the Pharaoh had not finished his lament.

"I invested all my savings in pyramids to secure a peaceful afterlife. But instead of enjoying eternal rest, I am plagued seven days a week by hordes of unwashed tourists. Thank Osiris, the mummies are well out of the way. At least I am spared their endless chatter about the latest embalming recipes."

As if to calm his troubled spirits, the Sakhmet Sisters now broke into song. It was a beautiful haunting tune. You could almost hear the lazy waves flopping onto the hot, sandy banks of the Nile and feel a fresh wind breathe new life into the limp sails of the feluccas. Gradually, the Pharaoh was carried back in time on the wings of their wonderful voices. The girls crooned and swooned in a way that suggested they were really rather fond of him. Amenophis III fell into a trance and even began to sing along with them.

"You can bongo on the Congo,
Sip cocoa on the Limpopo.
Or take it nice and easy
On the shores of the Zambezi.
But nothing beats the smile
Of a sunrise on the Nile."

It was all so wonderful they sang the last couplet again and again, each time getting fainter and fainter.

"But nothing beats the smile
Of a sunrise on the Nile."

After this, the two bears bowed and departed. The magical music of the Sakhmet Sisters followed them. Its rhythm entered their bones. Bodley swayed and danced as he walked. Even Bloomsbury bent a knee and tapped a foot in a most unbearlike manner.

When they were well out of earshot and could speak freely, Bloomsbury surprised Bodley by saying some very positive things about the song.

"If only we had really decent music like that nowadays. Wouldn't it be wonderful if the Sakhmet Sisters could make a comeback? Then everyone in the whole wide world could see and hear what it has been missing these past three millennia. What a sensation that would be. Just imagine."

LADY CARYATID

Bodley struggled along bravely to keep up with Bloomsbury. He was almost asleep on his feet. Then his ears picked up the echoes of the sweetest, loveliest sound he had ever heard. All of a sudden his fatigue melted away. He was miraculously revived, like he was walking on air. But he shivered at the unspeakable sadness expressed by the beautiful female voice uttered in a strange tone that was neither song nor speech. Just as the two bears turned a corner, the chanting stopped.

"Who disturbs my noble slumbers? Approach, strangers, and announce yourselves to Lady Caryatid of the Acropolis, lately of the city of Athens, Greece."

"Greetings, fairest Lady Caryatid, from your most devoted servant Bloomsbury. Also from my new acolyte Bodley, lately serving as academic underling to Professor Parchment in the city of Oxford, England."

Bodley stepped forward. He dared look no further than the lady's foot. Then his eyes followed the sweeping lines of a long robe carved from the finest marble. At last, his gaze was met by the gentle stare of a serenely beautiful face. A shaft of moonlight illuminated her lovely features.

"I bid you welcome. Professor Parchment is a good friend. True guardian of the ancient wisdom. Loyal keeper of the sacred flame. One of the few who still believes in us. He often comes to visit and writes fine things about us that sustain our fallen spirits through hard times. Without the likes of him I fear we should be quite forgotten. Then who would carry the memory of my sorry tale?"

Bodley waited with bated breath for Lady Caryatid to continue.

"Once I lived on the Acropolis in the metropolis of Athens with my five sisters. The six of us chatted contentedly from dawn to dusk, sometimes through the perfumed summer nights as well. Then one day a gang of rough, common labourers dismantled me and packed me in a wooden crate. I was helpless in their coarse hands. You should have witnessed the scene when they took me away. My sisters' tears flowed in a great torrent. Talk about the chorus of a Greek tragedy! The sea voyage to England was sheer torment. Now I am hidden away in this corner of the British Museum like an obscure object of shame."

Lady Caryatid paused for breath.

"Well, shame on the cursed one who brought me here. How I wish I had never been admired by that treacherous toad of an English aristocrat whose terrible name of Elgin I cannot mention without a stab of pain. Such indignities I have suffered at his hands. My heart's desire still yearns for the sun of Greece. My wet eyes dream always of the blue waves of the Aegean Sea."

Lady Caryatid stood there sobbing quietly under a shower of silvery moonbeams.

"Enough of that. What point in crying over lost glories? I am not the only one in here with a sad story to tell. Pray excuse my show of emotion. We Greeks do take things tragically. But we can laugh as well. I shall wear my comedy mask the next time you visit me."

As if to prove she could, Lady Caryatid put on a brave and beautiful smile.

"So now to the purpose of your visit. You have a question for me, I think?"

Bodley was quite unprepared for this. How did she know that? He was struck dumb with amazement. But there was no need for words.

"Say nothing. My divine intuition gives me the power to see deep into all mortal beings and read what is written in their hearts. I know what purpose has sent you to me. I know your question."

Bodley hung on her very word.

"You want to know who you are."

All Bodley could manage was a gulp followed by a silent nod.

"I can so easily give you the answer."

Bodley's heart thumped in his chest as he waited for Lady Caryatid to continue. Long seconds passed.

"But I won't speak yet. First you have to go on a journey. I see you making a long descent into a dark and dangerous place."

Bodley trembled.

"And then?"

"That is not revealed. But we shall meet again. So may Zeus be with you. I bid you good night."

Bodley's forebodings were lightened by the idea that they would meet again. Besides, he wasn't alone any more. He had Bloomsbury. His newly found friend and guardian was clearly on the best of terms with everyone worth knowing in the British Museum, from the Winged Lions of Nimrud to Amenophis III, the Sakhmet Sisters to the divine Lady Caryatid. All the same, he couldn't help wondering what was in store.

"What do you suppose she meant by that dark and dangerous journey?"

Bloomsbury hadn't liked the sound of that either. There was something ominous in the way she spoke. But he didn't want to alarm his young friend.

"Oh, I don't suppose she meant anything really bad. It's the sort of thing the Greeks generally say when talking of the future. Always full of doom and gloom."

With that Bloomsbury changed the subject.

"So I trust the company in here isn't too boring for your taste, young Bodley. You do see what I mean about statues having more to say for themselves than humans? There are plenty of others I want you to meet. We'll do the rounds properly tomorrow. I shall be most interested to hear what the Big Buddha has to say on the *Who am I?* question. He's the one to ask."

Who am I? Was it really so important to know? In fact, with every asking of the question the answer mattered less and less. Of all the people he had asked, Bodley reckoned only the lovely Lady Caryatid knew the truth. Or at least she was the one he wanted to hear the answer from. Somehow his true identity was safely lodged with her. That was enough for now.

Meanwhile, Bloomsbury navigated a complex roundabout route through the moonlit galleries filled with the strangest statues. Bodley avoided their blank, stony stares: far too tired for further conversations. At last, they reached the Round Reading Room. Bloomsbury opened a tiny door cleverly concealed behind a bookcase. They slipped through and closed it behind them. Then they climbed a long spiral stair and finally entered a small chamber tucked away behind the uppermost shelves under the great dome.

Bloomsbury sighed in the deep and satisfied way only bears can sigh when, after even the shortest absence, they set foot on home ground.

"Welcome, dear Bodley, to my delightful den, my cosy cave, my perfect *pied à terre*. Now it's time for a snooze, a nap, a siesta, a slumber, a doze, forty winks, a decent dose of Rip van Winkle or just a simple slee..."

Bloomsbury stopped in mid-word. Bodley had already curled up on the rug and was snoozing with utter ursine contentment. The older bear grunted his approval. No sooner had he donned his tasselled night-cap than his great brain fell into the silken embrace of sleep. Now they were both supping with the sandman, drowsing in the land of nod, scattering sleep dust along the dark highway of night, dreaming of who knows what. Perhaps of the Great Bear floating up there somewhere in the vast, star-spangled sky?

DEEP TROUBLE

Bodley awoke late the following morning. For a moment he had no clue where he was. No sign of Bloomsbury. He looked around. The walls of the room were lined entirely with shelves packed full of books. It felt like a prison. He shut his eyes and was immediately transported a long way off to lovely visions of flower-speckled meadows and the bubbling water of the river. How he ached to be with Cedric, Celia, Belinda and Victor Verum. He thought about them so hard he felt they must surely be right there with him. For one delicious moment it all seemed so real, he felt certain he was back in Oxford.

When he opened his eyes everything vanished in a flash. He must have been daydreaming. Perhaps even Bloomsbury was also a figment of his imagination? Yet the tasselled nightcap on the old brass bed wedged between two stout leather-bound volumes provided material proof of his friend's existence. Bodley took some comfort from this. Then he almost jumped out of his skin at the sound of a familiar voice.

"Awake at last, lazy-bones? A lot has happened and I simply must tell all. You are paying attention, *mon ami*, aren't you?"

Nothing could have delighted Bodley more than the sight of Victor Verum. But now he was sure he must be dreaming. How on earth could he be here? But there was the bookworm – real as daylight – perched on a bookshelf. How had the little fellow managed the trip from Oxford in such a short time? No need to ask, Victor was all too eager to fill in the details.

"After you left Duke Humfrey's, I was overcome by an irresistible urge to see the big, wide world. Seized by the great travel bug. Chronic case of *wanderlust*. Funny thing to happen to a bookworm. *Molto curioso*, don't you think?"

"Well, er ..."

"So, the very next day when Parchment showed up, I decided to follow in your footsteps. Burrowed deep into his manuscript and waited there until he stuffed the pages into his funny old bag. At last off he goes with *servitum vostrum* nicely tucked away inside. Just the same as you did. Daring stuff, don't you reckon?"

"Well, er ..."

"Then comes the bike ride. Rotten cyclist, or what? Straight through every pothole. Never out of second gear. Somehow we get to Amnesia Cottage. Must be named in his honour. Because he forgets all about the papers for a couple of hours. Finally, unpacks them and out I crawl, more dead than alive. So what do you think happens next?"

"Well, er ..."

"Meet a friend of yours. Neat bumblebee by the name of Belinda. Bit of a radical, but what a talker! I could hardly get a word in. What's happening to the world? Later on, I saw you come home, riding on a swan's back, if you please. You didn't see me. I was shut inside the house while you crashed out on the lawn. I wanted to get your attention, but I had to keep a low profile. Just think what Professor Parchment would do to a bookworm!"

Bodley took in every word of Victor Verum's breathless tale.

"Next morning, a nasty surprise. I'd just popped back into the manuscript for a quick snack when Parchment wraps it up in brown paper. Tough stuff. Totally indigestible. No way out. Could hardly breathe. Pitch dark inside. Trapped for ages. Much later, I heard an engine. Think it was a bus."

Bodley recalled the brown paper package with which he had shared the ride to London in Professor Parchment's bag. So Victor Verum had been his travel companion on the bus. If only he had known.

"What suffering. But all in a good cause. For when old Parchment eventually opened the parcel I found myself in the Round Reading Room of the British Museum. Paradise! A bookworm's dream! The ultimate challenge! Can you imagine what that means where I come from?"

Bodley stood there, speechless.

"I crawled out, overcome with excitement. But I had to hide until Parchment had gone. No idea where you were. Later on, I heard you crying. Came over to see what was the matter. But then Bloomsbury showed up. So I had to hide again. Almost laughed out loud when he came over all starry-eyed about those dusty old books of his. Never heard so much twaddle. But knew I had to keep well out of his way. He would never accept my eating habit, now would he?"

Bodley reflected that Victor Verum indeed had very good reason indeed to be wary of the book-loving Bloomsbury.

"So off you went the pair of you and I'm left all alone in the Round Reading Room. Spent the night snacking on this and that. Then slept until Bloomsbury started crashing about. That gave me the location of his den. Took me ages to get up here."

Victor Verum fell silent.

"What's that? I hear his footsteps. Help! Please don't tell Bloomsbury about me. Stand to. I'm coming aboard. You will keep mum, won't you?"

"Yes, of course, Victor. Mum's the word."

Bodley leaned forward and allowed the tiny bookworm to crawl from the bookcase and hide behind his left ear. At that very moment, Bloomsbury entered his den. Something was not quite as it should be.

"Who were you talking to just now, Bodley?"

The old bear looked about suspiciously.

"Well, er … no one. I was just doing some pon … ponticatifying, as a matter of fact."

"Pontificating, I think you mean. In which case I can only say well done, very well done indeed, my dear Bodley. Excellent effort! I started young too. Alphabet soup was my favourite when I was a cub. But pontificating is not as easy as it sounds. Takes plenty of practice. However, as a special favour to my newly appointed research assistant, I shall give you private tuition. You'll soon learn the ropes. Shouldn't take more than four to six hours practise a day and very soon you should be passably competent. In no more than three to five years, I dare say. Or thereabouts."

"But I can't spare three to five years, Bloomsbury. Or thereabouts. I want to go back to Oxford. Why don't you come too? You would love Amnesia Cottage. It's simply stuffed with books. Then there's the river. Have you ever done a trip on a swan's back? We could have so much fun."

"Fun, Bodley? Fun? Excuse me, but I don't see the point of fun. What about my researches and all this learning to be learned?"

"You can get all that in Oxford too."

The next words were whispered into Bodley's ear by Victor Verum.

"Tell Bloomsbury that the streets of Oxford are paved with learning."

The bookworm sounded quite excited.

"There is even one called Logic Lane."

Bodley relayed this information to Bloomsbury.

"Logic Lane? Am I hearing you right, Bodley?"

Bodley noted the magical effect this had on Bloomsbury. Suddenly he was agog with eagerness. Now was the time to press home his advantage.

"Yes, there is a Logic Lane and ...

But nothing came to mind. Luckily, the quick-witted bookworm helped out with another tempting name that Bodley dutifully repeated.

"… and an Algebra Alley."

"Algebra Alley? Oh my! How very interesting! What else?"

Bloomsbury's mind went into orbit, buzzing at the prospect of an entire city dedicated to intellectual matters. Just to keep him happy, Victor Verum supplied several suitable streets in swift succession: Symposium Circus, Grammar Grove and finally his trump card: Pontification Parade. Bodley relayed each in turn to Bloomsbury who repeated them with amazement and delight, as if he were being presented with the crown jewels. The last one went down particularly well.

"Pontification Parade? Oh my! Oh my!!"

In spite of all these riches Bloomsbury was wavering. Bodley wanted to give him yet more street names. But Victor Verum had run out of ideas. On his own, Bodley could only come up with Homework Hill and Rithmetic Road.

"Rithmetic Road, Bodley? Shouldn't that be Arithmetic?"

"Yes, of course, Bloomsbury. Actually, it's – thanks Victor – it's Arithmetic Avenue."

"What was that? Who is Victor? I don't see what this Victor has to do with it, whoever he is. So who is Victor, by the way?"

"Well, er no one in particular. Just a name that came into my head."

Bloomsbury eyed Bodley suspiciously.

"Indeed?"

So what do you say to Oxford?"

"Well, I must say Oxford sounds most appealing. But I should so miss being near the squares of my beloved Bloomsbury."

"But Oxford has plenty of squares too."

"You don't say?"

"Yes, hundreds of squares. There is one ... let me think ..."

Bodley racked his brains.

"Yes, there is one called Square Root Square."

Bodley could hardly believe he had come up with this one on his own.

"Square Root Square? Now, that does sound most exceedingly attractive!"

Bloomsbury was teetering on the brink of a momentous decision.

"Well, it's all very tempting, I must confess. But perhaps I am a bit too set in my ways to go gallivanting about the country."

Bodley received yet another prompt from Victor Verum.

"I say, Bloomsbury, did you know there is a pub in Oxford called *The Great Bear*?"

This proved to be the clincher.

"A hostelry called *The Great Bear*? You are quite sure about this, Bodley?"

"Yes, please say you'll come."

"*The Great Bear!* Why didn't you say so earlier? Let us be off. I see no point in delay."

Bloomsbury now bristled with excitement and anticipation. *The Great Bear!*

"Come along now, Bodley. Look lively. Let's be off. I trust you know the way to Oxford."

Bodley nodded a trifle uncertainly. He felt uneasy that he had elaborated a little. The name of the pub as supplied by Victor Verum was simply *The Bear*. Just to complicate matters, Bodley now realised he had not the foggiest idea how to get back to Oxford.

"Well, I know the way to Oxford Street. I saw it from the bus. So if we keep going in a straight line we should be in Oxford pretty soon, or thereabouts."

"Good, that's settled. Now I propose we take a quick tour through the Round Reading Room. We'll take a ride on a book barrow. I haven't done that for ages. I would like to say a proper farewell to the place. No knowing when I'll be back. *The Great Bear* indeed? Well I never!"

The two bears proceeded downstairs and climbed on to a barrow loaded with books. White slips of paper with the name of the person who had ordered each volume, stuck out. Bloomsbury examined them while they waited.

Several minutes passed without further comment. Bodley was dreaming of pleasures in store and a happy reunion with Cedric and Celia. At the same time he worried whether Oxford Street would really get them to Oxford. His thoughts were interrupted by a loud cry from Bloomsbury.

"I say! *Eureka! Eureka plus!* Look at the name on this slip of paper. Professor Parchment has ordered this book. Don't you see what this means, Bodley? He must be somewhere in the Round Reading Room. So to find him we just follow the book that will be delivered right to the desk where he is sitting. Then we simply stow away in his bag and ride off to Oxford in precisely the same way you arrived here. Easy as pie!"

The two bears hugged one another to celebrate their stroke of good fortune. For Victor Verum, still perched precariously behind Bodley's left ear, the proximity of Bloomsbury's muzzle was most alarming. The two bears danced a merry jig, which practically sent the bookworm tumbling out.

Seconds later, they rode triumphantly on the book barrow into the Round Reading Room. It soon found its way to where Professor Percival Parchment was working and the two bears hopped off onto the desk. From his flowing mane of snow-white hair and gold-rimmed, half-moon spectacles right down to his cracked leather shoes, the professor looked like a real scholar. The genuine article. Bloomsbury saluted him. But Parchment did not react. For Bloomsbury, just like Bodley, was invisible to humans.

Bloomsbury wanted to take a peep at the manuscript right away to find out what great discovery the professor was working on. But Bodley held him back, fearful lest he discover Victor Verum, who had just hidden away among the ink-spattered pages. So, the two bears crept quietly inside Professor Parchment's bag and waited for the ride to Oxford.

Professor Parchment, totally unaware of all these goings on, scribbled away in his manuscript with a great flourish. He was so pleased with himself he hummed and even whistled. This brought rasping coughs of disapproval and a sharp tap on the shoulder from another professorial personage sitting behind who gave him a polite ticking off for disturbing the peace.

Parchment took this as a cue to depart. He gathered the pages together and wrapped them once more in tough brown paper, which he tied securely with string. Then he muttered something about a lost world saved for posterity as he slipped the manuscript into the bag alongside the bears.

Bloomsbury patted the package with respect.

"A lost world saved for posterity, Bodley. Just imagine. Parchment must be on to something huge, and the secret is right here next to us inside this brown paper parcel. I can't wait to find out."

After that, they fell asleep. Time passed and they were some distance from the British Museum when they had a rough awakening. They felt themselves being swung about while travelling at great speed. In the distance they heard the distraught voice of Professor Parchment shouting for all he was worth.

"Stop thief! Stop thief! My life's work! Come back! Come back!"

But the thief sprinted on even faster. He paused when far enough ahead to shake the contents of the bag onto the ground. Along with the precious manuscript Bloomsbury and Bodley tumbled out like potatoes from a sack. The thief rummaged about feverishly only to discover there was nothing worth taking. So he abandoned his booty and raced off.

Professor Parchment now came lumbering breathlessly into view to retrieve his belongings. As he approached, the two bears stepped back smartly to avoid being trampled underfoot. Then something awful happened. As they toppled over backwards they were swallowed up by a big hole in the ground. They fell like two buckets down a well. It happened in a flash.

One moment Bloomsbury and Bodley were standing there. The next moment they weren't. It was as sudden as that. Gone!

IN THE DARK

The hole was bottomless. They dropped deeper and deeper until they surely couldn't drop any further. Any moment they expected to crash-land and break every bone in their bodies. But that didn't happen. Instead, they floated down gently on a cushion of warm air that billowed up from below. This was accompanied by a low growl arising from the bowels of the earth.

To their immense relief they made a soft landing. But where and on what they could not tell. Not a thing could be seen in the total darkness. Meanwhile, the growling noise faded away in the distance and gradually died altogether. Now it was pin-droppingly quiet. The two bears' noses twitched anxiously as each attempted to trace the whereabouts of the other.

Bodley's first thought was for Victor Verum. He looked about for a glimpse of those luminous green eyes. But there was no sign of his friend. He presumed the bookworm must have been carried off by the thief, trapped inside the package along with Professor Parchment's mysterious manuscript.

"Where are you, Bodley?"

"Over here, Bloomsbury."

"Just stay where you are. I'll be right over."

Paws extended in front of him, Bloomsbury inched his way forward.

"Got you!"

Bloomsbury's brain swiftly clicked into action.

"How long do you think we were falling? If we only knew that then I could perhaps work out how far down we are, and then …"

A distant rumble that became louder by the second interrupted Bloomsbury's mental arithmetic. A warm wind ruffled their fur. The growling increased in volume quite alarmingly. Bodley feared this might be some dreadful monster rushing towards them.

"It's an awful beast! Coming to eat us up! I'm so sorry, Bloomsbury. Really I am. I should never have asked you to leave the Round Reading Room. What a terrible mess I've got you into. Please forgive me!"

As for Bloomsbury he said nothing. Bravely, he pointed his snout into the wind that swelled in strength until it threatened to tear them apart. There would be no escaping whatever it was bearing down on them. The first sight of the monster confirmed their worst fears. Two cruel yellow eyes came racing toward them out of the darkness with murderous intent.

Bodley was tormented with guilt that he had misled his friend about those fancy streets in Oxford and even invented a pub called *The Great Bear*. To cap it all, he felt shame at his lack of courage as he cowered behind Bloomsbury. He recalled Lady Caryatid's dire prediction of this dangerous descent into a deep, dark place. She had said they would meet again. So surely all would be well? But it didn't seem like that. Not at all. A hurricane howled in their ears. The din was deafening. Any moment now, and it would be all over.

Still Bloomsbury stood there unmoved, rooted like a mighty oak tree, defiant to the end. Then, just when they expected to be knocked down and gobbled up, the roaring monster passed right over their heads. For several moments a hellish noise of thunder boomed in their ears. Then gradually it receded into the distance. How very strange. Stranger still, Bloomsbury's belly began to heave in spasms not of fright but of merriment. He was laughing.

Bodley didn't see the joke.

"Is it all over? Has the monster gone? I mean gone, as in really gone?"

Bodley's enquiry only triggered a fresh burst of mirth from Bloomsbury.

"Monster, Bodley? Some monster! What a pair of chumps we are. So glad I kept my eyes open. Do you want to know what that was? Nothing more terrible than the Cockfosters train. I read the destination sign just before it passed over us. Don't you see? We've fallen into the Piccadilly Line of the London Underground. Right in the middle of the track. Luckily we are under the rails. That is why nothing hit us. So all will be well if we keep our heads down."

This might have been delivered in ancient Greek for all the sense it made to Bodley. He stared after the red rear lights of the receding tube train as they slowly shrank until no bigger than cigarette ends. Then they were blotted out altogether. Inky blackness descended on them once more. Bloomsbury now presented his expert analysis of their predicament.

"This is just about the deepest hole in London we could have fallen into, Bodley. A ventilation shaft or suchlike. I reckon the air pushed out of the tunnel by that first train cushioned our fall. But there will be no such easy way back up out of here. So here we are, only the Great Bear knows how far from the nearest station. What to do? Perhaps we should sit down and think for a while? A spot of cool, concentrated cogitation usually does the trick."

So they sat in complete silence and tried to cogitate. They leaned on one another for comfort. It was just like being in a dark cave. Before long their minds drifted off into bearish thoughts of winter sleep.

"You know what, Bodley? I reckon a good long snooze is called for. Just like our forefathers out in the wild, we must lower our heartbeats to conserve energy. Then we shall feast on lovely memories of sunlit forests, golden honey flowing freely, lush red berries dripping from the bushes, silver salmon dancing in the river. After that ..."

Bloomsbury yawned. Already he was halfway back to ancestral dream-time. Then he rolled over and spoke no more. A deep snore arose.

Bodley sat there and listened. The snoring sounded so solid, almost like a physical object, heavy and immovable as the Rock of Gibraltar. He ruled out any thought of grabbing a snooze himself. He felt guiltier than ever he had deceived Bloomsbury into leaving his snug refuge in the British Museum. The least he could do was to guard his sleeping companion. He would stay awake and keep watch. But there was not a thing to watch. It was the darkest dark Bodley had ever seen. It was so dark he couldn't actually see the darkness. Impossible even to tell whether his eyes were open or shut.

He strained his ears to the utmost. But all he could hear was Bloomsbury's snoring, and the more he listened, the harder it became to resist the desire to fall asleep himself. Bodley's head rocked on his shoulders. Only a matter of time and he too would be out like a light. Then they would both be powerless. He yawned. His last resistance was ebbing away.

Just as Bodley was drifting off, something brought him smartly back to his senses. His acute hearing picked up a soft sound somewhere out there in the distance. It was no louder than the crackle of cereal in a china bowl, or the light scamper of birds' feet through dry leaves on a forest floor. Seconds passed in eerie silence. They seemed like minutes. Then the noise returned, slightly louder this time. More like the brittle chatter of knitting needles. No, it wasn't as harmless as that. A skeleton shaking its bones? He listened again. Whatever it was, was coming closer all the time.

Bodley gave Bloomsbury a sharp poke in the ribs. His snore wobbled for a moment then settled back into its previous steady rhythm. What was to be done? Bodley's next thought was to hide behind Bloomsbury as he had done before. But he immediately dismissed the idea as unworthy. He summoned all his courage. Now it was his turn to show what he was made of.

He stationed himself like an army sentry by Bloomsbury's side and stared towards the approaching noise. Now he could make out the faintest bluish-green glow in the inky gloom. It swayed to and fro like a handheld lantern. He could not tell how far away it was. It might have been a big light a long way off, or a tiny light just in front of him. He held his breath and waited.

Then, unexpectedly, the creature, whatever it was, began to sing. The tune was familiar, like that of *A Slow Boat to China*. But the words were different.

"I'm going to take you
Down the info super-highway
And out into cyberspace ..."

While repeating this refrain, the creature danced a slick soft shoe shuffle: three steps forward, one and a half steps back, before resuming its relentless forward advance. The mysterious bluish-green light came ever closer until it threatened to run smack into Bodley's shiny black nose. He held his breath. The light had stopped directly above him. Then the singing fell silent, rendering even louder the rumble of Bloomsbury's formidable snoring. Bodley sensed the creature's ears straining to listen. This was it. Time to face the music.

Suddenly, a voice began to speak.

"What on earth is that horrendously huge heap of fur? And what a frightful din it makes! I don't suppose it can be switched off?"

Bodley took exception to this. Immediately, he forgot his fear.

"That horrendously huge heap of fur happens to be my good friend Bloomsbury, who is in no mood to be switched off. Now pray tell me, whoever you are, what business you have to creep up on us in the dark without so much as a by-your-leave?"

Bodley regretted his bravado even as the rough words slipped off his tongue. He had only wanted to show he wasn't afraid. Now his fur stood on end while he awaited the creature's response. Long agonising moments passed. At last the icy silence was broken.

"I might well ask the same of you. This just happens to be my patch. I'm on my nightly patrol. Always do the rounds after the last train. If that isn't enough for your information, let me further advise you that my name is Russell. That's Russell as in Russell Square. Pride of the Piccadilly Line. My territory runs from here to Holborn. About to take over Covent Garden too. Keep that to yourself. Strictly shtumm, if you know what's good for you. So now tell me who you are and the nature of your business."

There was enough menace in the creature's voice to put a big dent in Bodley's new-found courage.

"Well, yes. Quite so. Of course, Mr Russell. My name is Bodley. That's Bodley as in Bodleian Library. My business? Well, in fact, I have no business down here. Neither does my good friend Bloomsbury, It's like this. We are lost in the dark and we are extremely desperate to find a way out."

"Extremely desperate are we, indeed?"

"Yes, Mr Russell. We are simply dying to get out of here, and I'm sure we will die if we don't. It's all been a nightmare. Professor Parchment was mugged and we fell down this gigantic hole. Then there was the monster. Now the darkness. It's horrible. You are our only hope. You must get us out of here Please!"

After a long and sinister pause, the creature spoke again.

"Horrible down here, is it? Well, I don't think so. Besides, you'll soon get used to the dark. So what's the big rush? If you want to know what's going on up top, just log on to the good old info super-highway, take a swing along the World Wide Web, or a nice long cruise through cyberspace. I surf the net whenever the mood grabs. Shall I check the opening prices on Wall Street? Cricket score from Down Under? I could e-mail a greeting to your folks, do a spot of electronic shopping, play chess with a Grand Master in Vladivostok, download a batch of files, create some macros, or get stuck into some serious digital interfacing. Then there's interactive multimedia and virtual reality. Not to mention network computer games. Or perhaps I should reformat my website? Hold on a moment. My modem is twitching. I'll be back in a half a nano."

None of this meant anything to Bodley. He would have asked Bloomsbury but his companion still showed not the slightest sign of waking. So he waited and waited while wondering what Russell could possibly be up to tapping away feverishly at his computer that gave off that eerie blue-green light.

"Like to have a look? I bet you would. With this mean machine I have the whole world in the palm of my paw. Gigabytes of ice cool technology. It has answers to everything. Even to questions you didn't know existed. I may be a complete scatterbrain, but with this little box of tricks, I'm an absolute genius. Thanks to this minuscule miracle, there's no need for me to know anything, except when I need to know it. Hey, that's good."

Russell now began to hum a tune of sorts. Then he broke into song.

"No need to know anything,
Except when I need to know it.
No need to go anywhere,
Except when I need to go it."

After this promising start, Russell's song tailed off and ground to a halt.

"Well, what do you say?"

"Very good, Mr Russell. Very musical."

"Musical? You bet I am! Ain't I just the coolest creature?"

Russell now performed a tricky dance routine on the steel rail.

"Just stick around, and you'll learn a thing or two. So how's about it?"

"How's about what?"

"Sticking around down here? Hanging out with me? Stuff like that."

"Actually, Mr Russell. Bloomsbury is the one to ask. He's in charge. I always go by what he says."

"Well, he doesn't have much to say for himself, does he? Unless that dreadful snoring is some kind of primitive language?"

"It's only heavy breathing. Bloomsbury has fallen asleep for a moment. When he wakes up you'll see what a clever head he has on his shoulders."

But Bloomsbury showed no sign of waking up. So Bodley poked him in the ribs, then tugged at his fur and finally shouted down his ear.

"I say, Bloomsbury, do wake up, please! There's someone here who can help us!! A Mr Russell!!! That's Russell, as in Russell Square!!!!"

All to no avail. Bloomsbury did not stir so much as a whisker. If anything, his snoring deepened. It was hopeless. There was no way of waking him.

With Bloomsbury fast asleep, Bodley had no choice but to ask for help.

"I say, Mr Russell, could you give me a hand waking Bloomsbury?"

Russell stared at the shapeless figure spread-eagled on the ground.

"Well, perhaps I could."

Then silence.

"Or, perhaps I couldn't."

More silence.

"I really don't see why I should."

"Please, Mr Russell."

"In any case, first I would need to know just what it is, this great snoring Bloomsbury thing."

"He's not a thing, Mr Russell. Bloomsbury is a bear, like myself."

"A bear? A bear, you say? Like you too? Well, I never. You are definitely in the wrong place, aren't you? Hold on and I'll see what I can find out."

More keyboard chatter ensued while Russell flicked through various menus.

"Bear. Got it. Large zoological item. Shaggy, flat-footed creature. Marked preference for hibernation. Hibernation? What's that?"

Russell clicked on *hibernation*.

"Hibernation. Goodness me! Spending the whole winter in a deep sleep. Is that right? Well, that seems clear enough. Your Bloomsbury is suffering from a severe case of hibernation. I think we'd best leave him alone until spring."

"But he can't be hibernating yet. We're still right in the middle of summer. At least we were yesterday. Or was it the day before yesterday? When I was out on the river in the sunshine with ..."

The words stuck in his throat. That idyllic day out in Oxford with Cedric and Celia was like the dream of an enchanted world lost forever.

"Yesterday, today, tomorrow. Makes no odds down here. And we don't bother with sunshine or seasons. Day, night, summer, winter. Who cares?"

"But Bloomsbury only said he was going to have a good long snooze."

"Well, just let him sleep it off then. In the meantime, there are miles of lovely dark tunnels to be explored. So let's get going."

As a last measure, Bodley tugged one more time at Bloomsbury for all he was worth. Then, against his deeper instincts, he kicked him as hard as he dared. But nothing would rouse him.

Finally, it was all too much for Bodley.

"Oh rats! And double-rats! This is a fine old mess I've got us into! But I won't leave you, my dear Bloomsbury. I promise I won't."

On account of the dark, Bodley failed to notice the immediate change in his sleeping companion. Bloomsbury's ears had twitched once at the mention of rats, then twice more at the mention of double-rats. A second later his eyes opened and he sprang with quite unexpected agility to his feet.

"Did I hear rats? What's all this talk about rats, Bodley? Rats are definitely the very worst thing to have in the proximity of one's ursine person in a decently organised den. So where are these pesky rodents? I'll soon sort them out."

Bloomsbury's threat would have been rather more convincing had he not been hopping about like a Scottish sword dancer.

"I didn't mean real rats. It was just a ..."

"Figure of speech or not. It's bad luck for bears even to mention rats."

Bloomsbury sniffed about suspiciously. Then he yawned a couple of times. He soon lost interest in the search for rats.

"Well, the rats must have gone. So I'll settle down for a bit more snooze. I don't know why, but I feel so frightfully fatigued down here."

With that, Bloomsbury yawned again, slumped to the ground and rolled over.

"No, Bloomsbury, please don't go back to sleep. We've got to get out of this place. Mr Russell here can help us. He's a very nice fellow."

But Bloomsbury was sinking fast.

"Well, do make sure your nice Mr Russell keeps the perishing rats away, won't you, Bodley?"

"But there are no perishing rats, Bloomsbury! Ask Mr Russell. This is his patch. I say, Mr Russell. Are you there, Mr Russell?"

It was now totally dark and silent but for Bloomsbury's snore like the engine of a lonely ship chugging through the middle of a trackless ocean. Then a sharp, angry voice pierced the black air.

"What makes you so sure there aren't any rats down here? I can summon a tidal wave of rats with just a single bleep on my modem. I'd like to see your fat friend's face when I introduce myself."

With that, the creature switched on his palmtop PC. He held it under his chin so that the light from the screen illuminated his features in the most scary way.

To his horror, Bodley now perceived that Mr Russell was a pointy-nosed fellow with small ears, long whiskers and very sharp teeth. A rat!

"Yes, my fine furry friend. Permit me to give you my full name. Rat! Russell Rat!! Mr Russell Rat!!! Mr Russell Perishing Rat!!!!"

This high-pitched outburst penetrated deep into Bloomsbury's dreams and triggered his alarm system. In a trice he was back on his feet and once more executing a feverish dance as if the very ground were seething with rodents.

"So the perishing rats have come back, have they, Bodley? Well, this is the best way to keep away from their sharp little gnashers. If I tread on one, so much the better, it will teach the others a lesson."

Bloomsbury persevered with his anti-rat hopping routine. But it was very heavy going. All those years in the Round Reading Room had done little for his fitness. He soon slowed to a plod and even that left him gasping for breath. Before long, he just stood there puffing and panting, looking anxiously at the ground, scarcely able to lift a foot.

"Well, Bodley. Quite a show I put on. Seems to have done the trick though, hasn't it? I reckon those pesky rodents must have cleared off."

Bodley tugged sharply at Bloomsbury's arm to draw his attention to Russell Rat who now began to speak in a most unpleasant manner.

"Pesky rodents? You had better learn some manners. But first, pray tell me from which troupe of flea-bitten dancing bears you have escaped. I expect your keepers will be anxious to have you returned."

Bloomsbury shook from head to foot at the sight of Russell Rat.

"*Rattus rattus!* Oh dear, Bodley, just what we need. Or rather, just what we don't need. A rampant specimen of *rattus rattus!* Oh dear, oh dear!"

"But, Mr Russell was just trying to explain ..."

"Quiet, Bodley. Leave this to me. Do you realise that ancestors of this knavish fellow, the dreaded black rat, spread bubonic plague all over Europe in the 14th century? Talk about perishing rats. This one is a real killer. Don't be fooled."

Russell immediately began a rapid search on his palmtop PC. A shriek of triumph announced he had found what he was looking for. He held the screen aloft for Bloomsbury to see.

"Hold it right there, you puffed up old bearskin! Not only are you arrogant and conceited but also an ignoramus of the first order. Kindly compare the two pictures. *Rattus rattus* aka the black rat is the one on the right. *Rattus norwegicus* aka the brown rat is on the left. I am of the latter species. I demand an apology, and make it a grovelling one, if you don't mind."

Bloomsbury might have responded in a more polite manner had not his intellectual capacity been called into question.

"Very well, *rattus norwegicus* or whatever you call yourself. It's too dark down here to tell the difference. When all's said and done, rats are rats. That's the end of it. The way I was brought up, bears simply don't talk to rats. Except to put them in their place. Which is sorely needed most of the time. That's the size of it. The long and the short of it. The top and the bottom of it, and the front and the back of it too. So there!"

"I see you are a very biased bear. Altogether unbearable. So there!"

"Have your little joke, ratbag. But that just proves my point. Unbearable has nothing to do with bears. Bearable, on the other hand, is what we are, denoting all that is easy to put up with, generally good and well worth the effort."

"But bears are smelly."

"Are they indeed? So why then does everyone say: I smell a rat?"

"That has no bearing on the matter."

Russell clicked away on his palmtop PC.

"Just listen to this, you bear with a sore head. The true definitions of bearish: *a) rough-mannered, b) generally pessimistic, c) tending to produce a fall in prices on the Stock Exchange.* Got that? Not much of a character reference, is it?"

"Quite preposterous, you ratfink. I've never been near the Stock Exchange."

"I don't suppose you have. Bears just sleep and do nothing. Hibernation, you call it? What a holiday! Meanwhile we rats are forever running about, always engaged in useful toil to keep the wheels of commerce and industry spinning. What, may I ask you, have lazy, useless bears ever contributed to the world?"

Bloomsbury, not used to being addressed in this manner, was momentarily speechless. Russell pressed home his advantage.

"I see I've got you well and truly rattled, you overbearing ..."

Bloomsbury now bounced back off the ropes.

"Overbearing? How can you ever have too much of a bear?"

"Well, I can see far too much bear right now."

"No need to get ratty. Besides, if rats are the first to leave a sinking ship, I wonder how you can live in this rat-hole? Answer me that!"

A tense silence fell while Bloomsbury and Russell searched for more verbal ammunition to carry on their war of words. Bodley despaired. How would they ever escape? Then he had a sudden flash of inspiration.

"Well, chaps. I'm delighted you are getting along so well. Just like a house on fire. I just knew you two would hit it off."

Bloomsbury and Russell both responded to this amazing suggestion with one voice.

"Getting along like a house on fire, are we? Hit it off, have we?"

"Yes, indeed. Do you realise you haven't stopped for breath?"

"Haven't stopped for breath? Haven't we?"

"Yes, and now you are both singing the same tune. So let's all shake on it to seal the friendship."

This turned out to be a real stroke of genius. For, without any hesitation, Russell generously extended a paw of peace. But it was only after much prodding from Bodley that Bloomsbury reluctantly responded with a paw outstretched in return. No sooner was the deed done than the rodent immediately became the friendliest of companions.

"No hard feelings, Bloomers old pal? So now the formalities are dealt with, please consider yourselves my very special guests down here. I'll do you a guided tour, show you the sights, roll out the red carpet, introduce you to my cronies. I have lots of mates. Simply squillions of ratty pals. All very hard working members of society. Unlike some I could mention."

Bloomsbury was about to renew the rat versus bear debate, but then thought better of it. The prospect of a close encounter with simply squillions of rodents left him in a high state of ursine alarm.

"Why so silent, Bloomers? We're going to have ourselves some serious fun. Let's hit the town. There's bound to be a rave on somewhere."

Bloomsbury finally regained the power of speech. He hadn't a clue what a rave was. But he knew as sure as bears are bears that he wouldn't like it.

"A rave, Russell? Please don't trouble yourself, my good fellow. I'm not much of a night owl, and it's way past Bodley's bedtime."

Russell waved aside the objection. Bloomsbury whispered in Bodley's ear.

"A rave? Can't say I like the sound of that. Would have been better if we hadn't made friends so quickly. Might be all right for rats to change their tune at the drop of a hat. But we bears are generally more constant in our emotions than these fickle rodents. Why, there are some folk I've disliked for years without knowing why or even thinking about it. But at least I have been consistent. Don't know what came over me just now, making friends with a rat. I'm behaving quite unlike myself, and I can't think why."

"But Russell isn't such a bad fellow."

"Perhaps he isn't. But the thought of meeting squillions of his rat pals gives me an almighty itch and shiver under the fur."

After another flourish on the keyboard, Russell snapped shut his palmtop PC and slipped it into his waistcoat pocket. The tiny computer fascinated Bodley.

"Does it know everything, your machine?"

"Sure does. Whatever you want. Whenever you want. Just ask it anything."

In spite of his resolve not to, Bodley couldn't help but ask his question. It sort of asked itself before he could stop it.

"Can it tell me who I am?"

"Who you are? Are you serious? Don't think the search engine can deal with stuff like that. But I guess the data must be in here somewhere. I'll have a go later. Right now we must be hitting the trail. Tell you what, you can ask in the Rat Race. That's where the rave is. The guys there are well wired up. They can fill you in on whoever, whatever, wherever, whenever. They have answers to questions you wouldn't even know how to ask. The Rat Race is where the action is, pretty cool, well wicked, a class joint. Climb up and we can skate along the live rail. Don't worry. They've switched off the juice for the night. I'll have us there in two shakes of a rat's tail. Get it, Bloomers old sport? Two shakes of a ... Oh, never mind, the night is young. My whiskers are twitching. Let's go raving. Come along now, you lost pair of bears, and don't forget your luggage."

"I don't think we have any luggage, do we Bloomsbury?"

"Indeed not. We didn't exactly prepare for this trip, now did we Bodley?"

Bodley smarted at the reproach in Bloomsbury's voice. He was glad the dark hid his embarrassment. Russell hurried them up.

"OK, let's get going. Just follow me, Bloomers. You'll soon get the hang of it."

Obediently, they fell into line. Anything was better than being left all on their own in that dark, forbidding place. As Russell had promised, they found the going easy enough on the mirror-smooth surface of the shiny steel rail. They glided along behind the rat, who set a brisk pace. Bodley, bringing up the rear, gave Bloomsbury a nudge every now and then to help him on his way.

"I say, Bodley. This live-rail skating is a most unconventional and unbecoming mode of locomotion."

As they skated along, Russell began to sing once more in that curious high-pitched voice of his.

"I'm going to take you
Down the info super-highway
And out into cyberspace..."

Bodley sang along to the refrain but Bloomsbury did not join in. He feared nothing but trouble could possibly come of this foolhardy escapade. To add insult to injury, being addressed as Bloomers by a smart alec rodent was strictly out of order. But what was he to do? If ever a spot of cool, concentrated cogitation was called for, it was now. It was now.

"I dread to think what we shall find in this Rat Race place. May the Great Bear protect us."

When they reached Holborn, Russell led them up onto the platform.

"All change for the Central Line."

First, they had to climb a long escalator that had been switched off for the night. Russell skipped up the steep steps quite easily. Bodley managed well enough too. But for Bloomsbury it was a tough struggle.

"Must we really go to this Rat Race place? Can't we go raving some other time? Tomorrow perhaps when I've got my breath back?"

"Come on, Bloomers. The night is young."

Bloomsbury felt anything but young at that moment. But there was no arguing with Russell. Soon the rat had them gliding smoothly along on yet another polished live rail. Now they were heading east on the Central Line. How far they had travelled, they couldn't tell. Suddenly, Russell hissed at them to stop.

"The Rat Race. We're here."

The two bears looked apprehensively into the gloom. Straining their eyes they could just make out what looked like the platform of a deserted station. It was even spookier than the tunnel.

"Better let me go first."

Russell pushed open a small door to release a sudden flood of glaring red and yellow light. Deafening decibels of throbbing techno music hit their ears.

Bloomsbury recoiled.

"I'm not too sure about this, Bodley. Let's beat a retreat while we still have time."

Too late. Russell was already ushering them in.

"I say, Russell, perhaps if we just poked our noses round the door and came away smartly, eh? I'm sure that would give us the general idea."

"Don't worry, Bloomers, old pal. No probs when you're with Russell, OK? Just stick close, and you'll connect. The Rat Race is a high-tech, state-of-the-art, cosmopolitan, global networking environment with simply the coolest communications co-ordinates and the fastest pentium processors in town. The most sophisticated peripherals, too. Even the modcons fully digitised. Strictly the best for upwardly mobile rodents. All top ranking rats come here: plutocrats, autocrats, meritocrats, bureaucrats, technocrats. Even aristocrats and democrats, you name it."

"Sewer rats too, I shouldn't be surprised."

The ecstatic Russell did not hear this remark.

"Bet you bears have seen nothing like this."

Indeed, they had not. The Rat Race was like being inside a computer with electronic circuit boards, metal wires and microchips everywhere you looked. Flashes of data reeled past faster than you could possibly read them on batteries of TV monitors. The ceiling blazed with strobe lights and the wall sported digital clocks giving the time in New York, Tokyo, London and Frankfurt. The bar extended for miles, with sharp-elbowed rodents occupying every inch of the long counter. The men in dark shirts and bright ties waved gold credit cards. The women in sexy dresses swung shiny handbags stuffed with wads of bank notes. No sooner did one rat get a drink than another took its place. Russell had to shout to make himself heard above the braying of drunken voices all talking at once. Some were chanting *bonuses, bonuses!*. It was sheer bedlam.

"Friday night fever. End of the week. Markets shut tomorrow. You'll never believe how much booze these guys and girls get through. Flashing cash like there's no tomorrow. Fast-track mega-bucks. Simply incredible! Don't you think it's the wildest, wackiest, wickedest place on planet earth?"

Russell pointed to a big overhead screen that brought frantic images of wars, accidents, demos, crimes, disasters and suffering from around the world. Every few seconds the station logo flashed into life.

WELCOME TO NONSTOP NEWS FROM TOTAL TV. THE CHANNEL WHERE BAD NEWS IS GOOD NEWS. GREAT ENTERTAINMENT TOO WITH SOMETHING AWFUL HAPPENING SOMEWHERE. MAKE SURE YOU SEE IT FIRST ON TOTAL TV. STAY TUNED. COMING UP NEXT OUR TOP STORIES. EVERYTHING FROM TYPHOONS AND TIDAL WAVES TO TRAIN CRASHES AND TERRORISM. ALL BROUGHT TO YOU IN THE COMFORT OF YOUR OWN HOME BY NONSTOP NEWS FROM TOTAL TV.

There was also a smaller screen in the shape of a sleek flat monitor. It consisted simply of a four-figure number that changed every couple of seconds like a taximeter. No indication what it was meant to be, except for the two capital letters GI spread across a spinning globe positioned directly above it.

Russell led them away from the noise to a secluded corner.

"That, pals, is the good old GI. That's GI as in the Global Index. It's what makes the world go round. Keeps the poles cold, the equator hot, and generally holds the hemispheres together."

The two bears stared at these all-powerful electronic digits. They noted that every client of the Rat Race glanced up every few seconds at them, as if for reassurance that all was well with the Global Index.

Russell explained.

"The GI is the mother of them all. Dow Jones, Footsie, Nasdaq and Nikkei rolled into one, along with Paris, Zurich, Hong Kong and the rest. All oil reserves, gold bars, diamonds, real estate, cash, postal orders and premium bonds in existence. The combined value of every last thing from the Empire State Building down to that forgotten packet of peas at the bottom of your freezer, all added together at the latest market prices. The good old GI tells us exactly how much at any moment the world is actually worth."

The two bears shook their heads slowly. Bloomsbury had a perplexed look on his face as he tried to come to grips with the concept.

"What the world is worth, you say, Russell? I really don't see the point of that. Perhaps if someone wanted to buy the world, then I just suppose there might be some sense in it. But even then not much."

"Cool thinking, Bloomers. Hole in one. Imagine the scenario. Just suppose an alien from outer space wanted to purchase Planet Earth. Lock, stock and barrel. Well, we'd look pretty silly if we didn't know our market spot price. Remember how the Red Indians were ripped off when they sold Manhattan to the Dutch for a paltry handful of cheap glass beads."

Economics was not Bloomsbury's strong point, but he prided himself on being able to fathom most matters. Here, however, he was completely out of his depth. He showed his frustration by raising his voice.

"So who do you think is going to buy the world? The man in the moon?"

Now Bloomsbury was not to be stopped.

"If you want my opinion, this Global Index thing of yours is absolute poppycock, total and utter rubbish, a piece of the most far-fetched foolishness! As for your clever computers, give me a real bear brain any time for a spot of cool, concentrated cogitation."

Russell was quick on the counter-attack.

"That's just typical of you bears to run down what you don't understand. No wonder you haven't left your caves, while we rats can tell you exactly what the world is worth, cash on the nail, and seasonally adjusted too!"

At this, several rats turned to observe one of their own kind in dispute with a gruff old bear. As word spread, Bloomsbury and Bodley were hemmed in by a squirming multitude of rats. The rodents were in angry mood. Bears were strictly bad news. Markets hated bears. The rats hissed at them and showed their sharp teeth. Bodley grew alarmed. Only Russell could save them from imminent doom. But even his cheery bluster was wearing thin.

"Cool it, guys. I was only showing these ursine primitives what miracles we rats have achieved. Just look at the value we keep putting on the GI through our enterprise. Without us, the world would be quite worthless. Surely we can afford to be tolerant of an inferior species?"

At this, Bloomsbury stood up.

"Inferior species? I really can't let that insult pass undisputed!"

Whiskers twitched and teeth flashed at the shocking sight of a bear standing on its hind legs in the Rat Race. A ripple of alarm spread through the crowd and surged back vastly amplified. The Global Index had stopped its rise. Next, it wobbled a bit before going into decline. Suddenly, it was in free fall. Panic spread. Mobile phones were snatched from pockets and everyone rushed for the exit. Within seconds, the Rat Race was as deserted as the Marie Celeste. In the ensuing silence they heard an announcement.

TOTAL TV INTERRUPTS THIS BULLETIN OF NON-STOP NEWS FOR A NEWS FLASH. THE GLOBAL INDEX HAS NOSEDIVED. BILLIONS WIPED OFF THE VALUE OF THE WORLD. IF THE PANIC CONTINUES, PLANET EARTH

WILL SOON BE WORTH LESS THAN A PACKET OF SALTED CRISPS. WITHOUT THE SALT. OUR TOTAL TV TEAM IS ON ITS WAY TO THE RAT RACE WHERE THE TROUBLE STARTED. STAY TUNED FOR OUR STORY UPDATE.

Russell and Bodley stared blankly at the screen. Bloomsbury looked pretty pleased with himself.

"Well, Russell. So much for the value of rodent civilisation. Just goes to show that your ratty world isn't worth as much as you thought it was."

Poor Russell for once had nothing to say. To make matters even worse Bloomsbury gloated over his unexpected triumph.

"Now you can see what one lone bear can achieve simply by being bearish."

Bodley looked about anxiously.

"Don't you think we should get out of here? The party seems to be over, well and truly. Heaven knows what will happen next."

Bloomsbury, still full of himself, led the way out. Bodley and Russell trailed numbly in his wake. As they left by the side door a film crew from TOTAL TV stormed in through the front. Already, a reporter was doing a piece to camera against the backdrop of the deserted Rat Race and the plummeting Global Index.

Russell quickly realised the full danger of the situation. Outraged at the collapse of their sacred Global Index, every last angry rat in the London Underground would be after the bears. More to the point, after him. They would have his guts for garters. He'd done some foolish things in his time, but taking two bears to the Rat Race really took the biscuit. Now he had no choice but to escape with Bloomsbury and Bodley back to the upper world and then lie low until things cooled down. Survival instinct told him to head first for his own patch where he knew every last nook and cranny.

"Hurry. Hurry. Get your skates on. We've got to get back to Russell Square."

Soon the three fugitives were skating along the live rail of the Central Line back to Holborn as fast as they could go. Then they tumbled down the immobile escalator and raced along to the Piccadilly Line.

"Get a move on. They won't be far behind."

As they slid through the tunnel they could hear the excited squealing of at least a thousand rats closing in on them in the darkness. At last they reached Russell Square. They scrambled up onto the platform. Russell sprinted nimbly ahead, while Bodley lagged behind to help Bloomsbury who was close to dropping. His body refused to go any further. He dragged himself up to a landing where he collapsed in a panting heap of fur.

Russell looked anxiously over his shoulder while Bodley made a forlorn effort to help him to his feet

"One last big effort, Bloomsbury. The rats are coming. I can hear them."

Bloomsbury looked despairingly at the staircase. It curled up and away in a broad spiral. He groaned with dismay as he read a notice.

THIS STAIRWAY HAS 175 STEPS. DO NOT USE EXCEPT IN AN EMERGENCY

It was an emergency all right. But Bloomsbury couldn't manage another step, let alone 175. Yet somehow, he rallied his strength for a final speech.

"Save yourselves. It's me they're after. My time is almost up in any case. I've had a good innings. I didn't meet the Great Bear in this life but there's always the next. Just think I was the bear who made a right old pickle of the Global Index. So farewell, my friends. Don't give up the pontificating, Bodley. You show such promise. Russell will take care of you. Now scarper, vamoose! Be off the pair of you!"

It was a brave speech. But they took no notice of it. Bodley did not budge from Bloomsbury's side. Nor did Russell scarper or vamoose, even though the rats were closing in fast. In less than a minute the angry rodents would be upon them. Vital moments ticked away. It looked hopeless. Then, as if by a miracle, something happened. The cold metal wall behind them made a great jolt and a shudder. Two seconds later, a set of steel doors slid back. The lift had been switched on. The timing could not have been better.

Bodley and Russell dragged the thoroughly exhausted Bloomsbury inside. It took ages before the doors closed behind them. At last they were whisked up and away out of danger in the nick of time. Rats were now swarming in vast numbers out of the tunnel and along the platform of Russell Square. The lift delivered the trio swiftly back into the welcome dawn of the upper world. They staggered out into Bernard Street. Bloomsbury, who had never had such a hair-raising adventure before, was relieved beyond measure.

"I must thank you most sincerely, my dear Russell. You really saved our bacon."

Russell knew it wasn't over. Far from it. The rats were after his blood and wouldn't give up easily. He had broken every rule in the rodent code and betrayed his own kind by siding with the arch enemy. To mask his anxieties, Russell preened his whiskers and placed some trendy sunshades on his nose at a rather jaunty angle. He admired his reflection in a shop window.

Meanwhile, behind this casual show of ratty nonchalance Russell's brain went into overdrive. He ran through the likely scenarios. He didn't think the rats would come after them in broad daylight. At least not immediately. First there would be an emergency session of the Rodent High Security Council. But come they would, though it was impossible to say exactly how or when they would strike back and take their revenge.

The three companions held their breath, looked and listened to make sure the coast was clear before they ventured out into the deserted early morning streets. A broad green dome arose above the lofty plane trees of Russell Square. Bloomsbury stopped and raised his arms in awe and wonderment.

"What a glorious sight! Home sweet home! The Round Reading Room! That's where we'll go. They won't think of looking for you there, Russell."

Russell still felt uneasy.

"Maybe so. But better take a detour. Just to make sure we aren't being followed. Don't want them to know where we're going."

So they headed north. Minutes later they arrived at Tavistock Square. Right in the middle of the garden there was a bronze statue of an old man sitting on a stone plinth. He was clad only in a scanty cotton garment quite unsuited to the London climate. Bloomsbury took care of the introductions.

"This, my friends, is Mahatma Gandhi. Small in stature, but a most remarkable Indian gentleman. His head contains more wisdom than the whole of the Bloomsbury Group put together. Let's ask his advice."

Suddenly, they were startled by a blood-curdling bark. They turned to face an enormous Rottweiler homing in on them with bared fangs.

"Quick, follow me. There's a small hiding place under the statue. Quick!"

They scampered after Russell into a cave-like opening at the base of the plinth. They cowered inside with their backs pressed up against the stone wall. The Rottweiler, seeing it had them cornered, circled the statue a couple of times before pushing its moist snout towards them. Russell gave it a sharp bite. The dog yelped with pain, sprang back but soon advanced again with a deadly snarl. Bloomsbury was alarmed.

"Do you really think it was a good idea to upset him like that, Russell? I reckon I can make the dumb brute understand that its unprovoked aggression is quite pointless and altogether counter productive."

Bloomsbury didn't get a chance to try his theory on the vicious dog, which now advanced a tentative paw to winkle them out. Russell and Bodley wriggled free of its clutches. But Bloomsbury was caught by his braces. He gave a sorry look of total despair as he was slowly dragged out. Bodley grabbed him by the ankles and tried for all he was worth to pull him back to safety.

He called to Russell to lend a hand. But the rat was nowhere to be seen. It was an unequal struggle. Steadily, the Rottweiler reeled them both in. It looked very pleased with its prize catch of two plump bears.

Bodley overcame all fear in the heat of battle. He was determined to do the right thing and stick with his friend to the bitter end.

"Looks like we're on our own, Bloomsbury. But I won't let go of you. I promise I won't."

Just when all seemed utterly lost and hopeless the vicious salivating hound suddenly let out a piercing yelp and jumped several feet in the air, releasing Bloomsbury and Bodley in the process.

"Yes, you great slobbering brute, I gave you that bite in the bum. But if you want to make a fight of it, you'll have to catch me first."

Russell scampered off with the outraged hound yapping at his heels so intent on its prey it couldn't see beyond the end of its snout. It followed blindly as Russell entered the open gate of a fenced compound only to slip out through the iron railings on the far side. But where the slim rat had passed like a dose of salts the fat dog could not follow. Unable to stop, the brute crashed muzzle first into the metal bars. It slumped to the ground and lay there in a daze, seeing an entire galaxy of stars. Quick as a flash, Russell shut the gate behind the unconscious Rottweiler and slid the bolt. He doubled back to his friends still cowering in the hollow beneath Mahatma Gandhi's statue.

"Come quickly, the stupid beast has knocked himself out. I've got him caged up like a pig in a pen."

The owner of the Rottweiler now arrived on the scene. The man went over to release his precious pet. In puzzlement he scratched his head with one hand while the other dangled an empty leash.

"So there you are, Reginald. What on earth have you been chasing? There aren't any rabbits in Tavistock Square. And can't you read, you silly chap? That's a dog free area you're in. You've more bark than brains. I'll have to put you back on the lead."

The three companions headed directly for the safety of the British Museum. Reginald Rottweiler, a bit unsteady on his paws, came trailing along not far behind. He was limping sullenly at the end of a leash. When the dog saw them it lunged forward. But his owner restrained him.

"Come along now, Reginald. Enough of all that barking and growling. There's nothing there. Any more tantrums and you'll not get any lunch today."

So the hound from hell allowed himself to be led off meekly in total humiliation while the fugitives made good their escape. Just then two fat pigeons waddled over. Out of idle curiosity they had followed the action all the way from Tavistock Square.

"All go this mornin', Fred?"

"Pourin' bears, rats and dogs, Joe."

"A right old game of soldiers, innit?"

"You're tellin' me."

Bloomsbury glanced over his shoulder. Then he led Bodley and Russell through a secret entrance into the British Museum. But a sharp-eyed rodent scout had spotted them and immediately scuttled off to tell his ratty friends what he had observed.

NARROW ESCAPE

Once inside the British Museum, the two bears and a rat made straight for the Round Reading Room. No sooner did they reach Bloomsbury's den than they immediately fell asleep. They were absolutely all in after their all-night adventures.

It was mid-morning before they stirred. Russell was the first to open his eyes. He rapidly surveyed the unfamiliar surroundings. Bloomsbury's book-lined retreat could have been designed for a crusty professor from the Victorian era. It was so cluttered, shabby and old-fashioned, nothing like the sleek, modern setting he was used too. He felt completely out of his element.

Bodley now awoke and peered out through the gap between the books that served as Bloomsbury's window down onto the Round Reading Room. The big clock below indicated a quarter to eleven.

"Gosh, is that the time? Hope we aren't too late to catch the Prof ..."

His unspoken words tailed off as he recalled the catastrophic events of the previous day and night. No doubt Professor Parchment was already back home at Amnesia Cottage, Oblivion Avenue, Oxford. Bodley's thoughts now turned to Victor Verum. What chance would the tiny bookworm have in the hands of the ruthless criminal who had stolen the Parchment Papers? Very slim indeed. Even so, Bodley hoped it was just possible Parchment might have managed to retrieve his manuscript from the thief. In which case, the best place to look for Victor was surely to track down the Professor and then ... But there were too many missing pieces in the puzzle.

At that moment Bloomsbury yawned, stretched, yawned again and rubbed the sleep dust from his eyes.

"Good morning, gentlemen. I trust you spent a comfortable night. Now where were we? Ah, yes. As I was about to say back there in Tavistock Square when I was so rudely interrupted by that ridiculous rottweiler called Reginald. There are plenty of loose ends to be tied up."

Russell still couldn't get over the olde worlde atmosphere that breathed out of very object in Bloomsbury's den. It was a real culture shock.

"Your place is just like a museum, Bloomers!"

Bodley thought Bloomsbury would explode. Instead, he beamed with pride.

"A museum? Why, thank you very much, my dear Russell. Most kind of you to say so. I am glad it is to your satisfaction. But I can't take all the credit. For this is the way bears are supposed to live. Besides, as a tenant of the British Museum I have to maintain the proper standards."

"No, Bloomers. What I mean is, why don't you get your pad made over? Throw out all this old clutter. How can you possibly live like this?"

"My pad? Old clutter? I don't know what you're talking about. I beg to inform you again this is precisely how bears are meant to live."

126

"Well, give me the Rat Race any day. And just look at your old tweed jacket and those grey flannel trousers. No one wears gear like that any more."

"Well, I do!"

"Well, if that's your idea of fashion, I can't see much future in being a bear."

Bodley felt uneasy. This was a very bad start to the day. Considering the serious dangers they faced, shouldn't they all pull together? This bickering wouldn't help. He feared the unresolved rats vs bears debate was about to recommence in earnest as Bloomsbury now fired a salvo in return.

"Future, my dear Russell? The future will come one way or another. With or without rats. Call me old fashioned. But since tomorrow's fashion is simply yesterday's mode recycled, I merely have to wait for things to come round. I may be like a clock that has stopped. But at least I tell the correct time twice a day. So I am always ahead of the times just as much as I am behind them."

"You, ahead of the times? In what way? Just give me one example!"

"Just one example, you say? Why just one? I bet you there are so many things I know of from the distant past that were way ahead of what is happening now. If they could be rediscovered then they would be the very height of fashion all over again."

"Things? What things?"

"Things I happen to know about and you don't."

127

Russell was getting annoyed with Bloomsbury dodging the question.

"Things? Like what things? Just give me one single example, and the bet is on, Bloomers."

"Bet? Did I say bet?"

"Yes, you did. Are you backing out?"

Things were moving far too fast for Bloomsbury. He hadn't meant to place a real bet. Like practically everything he said, it was just a manner of speaking not to be taken literally. But now he had said it, he couldn't back down and lose face. The honour of bears was at stake. So he had to think of something to bet on. Suddenly, he recalled what he had said about how splendid it would be if the sizzling Sakhmet Sisters could be rediscovered.

"Well, let me predict for example that an ancient Egyptian girl band is about to take the world by storm. Become pretty hot stuff, make it serious big time, as I expect you and your rat pals would say."

"Not good enough, Bloomers. Far too vague. You must name names."

"Very well. They are the Sakhmet Sisters."

"The Sakhmet Sisters? Never heard of them."

"Precisely my point. They were famous once but are unknown now. Though not for long."

"OK. So when will these Sakhmet Sisters of yours make it big time?"

"Oh, that's not so easy to say."

"Well take a guess."

"Pretty soon. In a few days. Or thereabouts."

"OK. I'll give them to the end of the week and the bet is on. So what are the stakes? Tell you what, I'll wager my palmtop PC against your ..."

Russell looked about in vain for something in Bloomsbury's den or on his person he wanted to possess. There was absolutely nothing.

"Very well, Russell. Your palmtop thingamajig – whatever use that can possibly be to me I don't know – against all my academic research notes. A world of wisdom against an empty machine. I can't be fairer than that. The bet is on. Let's shake on it."

The last thing Russell wanted was Bloomsbury's research notes. But a bet was a bet. So they shook on it. Bloomsbury had never wagered anything before and the thrill put him in high spirits.

"Well, that's settled, and now I propose a cup of tea to activate the brain cells. Then we shall get down to business. My humble abode may not be the last word in fashionable modernity. But I think I can brew up a very passable imitation of an excellent pot of tea."

In contrast to Bloomsbury's breezy mood, Russell had lost his habitual jaunty optimism. Fearing he might possibly be about to lose his precious palmtop PC, he flicked it open to run a rapid search for the Sakhmet Sisters. The name didn't figure on any of the current gigs listings. They must be total unknowns. He breathed a sigh of relief. They couldn't possibly come from complete obscurity to mega stardom in a few days. Or could they?

Bloomsbury eyed Russell suspiciously.

"Why do you have to consult that machine every time you want to know something, Russell? Don't you have a brain in that head of yours?"

Russell did not respond to the taunt. He had just clicked on the home page of *www.rattyworldnews.com* and a huge picture of himself suddenly filled his PC screen. He scrolled down for further info. A text detailed his unforgivable crimes of economic sabotage against the Global Index, also conspiring with two bears to escape justice. He was an outlaw!

A popup screen showed his picture, covered with large, red letters dripping with blood.

WANTED URGENTLY. DEAD OR ALIVE. RUSSELL RAT. HUGE REWARD.

Russell's heart froze. He was a rat on the run and had been wasting precious time making silly bets with bears while his life was in danger. Now his whiskers began to twitch in a most alarming way. This was a warning signal that invariably spelled trouble.

Seconds later, Russell knew exactly what sort of trouble. Through the gap in the bookshelf he surveyed the scene down below. The Round Reading Room had not yet opened for the day, but already it was a hive of activity. The whole place seethed with rats. Thousands of rodents were on the rampage, swarming all over the desks and shelves, sticking pointed noses and sensitive whiskers into every tiny nook, investigating every little cranny. They were hot on his trail.

He conveyed the bad news to the two bears.

"We've been rumbled. Afraid we'll have to skip the tea party for now, Bloomers. The rats are here."

Bloomsbury peeped out to see for himself.

"Good lord! The Round Reading Room invaded by a regiment of rodents! Heaven preserve us from their nasty little gnashers!"

Instinctively, Russell defended his own kind.

"Easy, Bloomers. We're not such a bad bunch. But after what you did to the Global Index, anything is possible. Where money is concerned, rats never want to miss a trick. They don't take kindly to losing out."

They could see Russell's divided loyalties. It was really all their fault for landing him in this impossible situation. Bloomsbury cogitated. For a while, no one spoke. Then Bodley put in a word.

"Isn't there somewhere we can hide?"

At long last Bloomsbury spoke.

"There's a huge bronze bell over by the statue of the Big Buddha. We can slip inside a small hole at the back and hide there until the dust has settled. A secret passage will get us nearly all of the way there without being spotted. It's our best and only chance."

For want of a better plan, they let Bloomsbury lead them. So off they went down the spiral stair behind the bookcase. They slipped undetected into a labyrinth of tunnels spreading in all directions under the floor of the British Museum. Without Bloomsbury to guide them, Russell and Bodley would have been lost in an instant. So they followed his every step as he charted an amazingly complicated route through this subterranean maze. Every now and then the old bear stopped to listen for the faintest sound of rats' paws up above and scratch his wise head before continuing. Not a word was spoken until they arrived at an air vent in a corner of the Egyptian Gallery. Bloomsbury told them in a solemn whisper they would now have to take a chance and cross an open space above ground.

They didn't get far before they were spotted by a couple of rats. Russell immediately assumed command. He pushed the two bears behind a pillar and boldly stepped forward to challenge his fellow rodents.

"Here I am! It's me you're after. But you'll have to catch me first."

Russell scurried off with the two rats on his tail. Seconds later, a great hue and cry went up as the entire invasion of rats joined in the chase. A torrent of rodents flooded past the two bears, safely hidden behind the pillar. They were totally overlooked in the general confusion. Bodley heaved with a burning desire to rush out and do something, if only to create a diversion and take the heat off Russell. But Bloomsbury held him back.

"No, we can't help Russell just like that. A spot of cool, concentrated cogitation is all that can save us now. So think, Bodley. Think."

Long seconds passed in silence. Bodley tried to think. Suddenly he thought about the last thing Russell had said. About rats never wanting to miss a trick where money is concerned. He whispered this to Bloomsbury who repeated the words to tease out the germ of a plan that was beginning to form.

"Rats never want to miss a trick where money is concerned. You're absolutely right, Bodley. He did say that, didn't he?"

Bloomsbury weighed the words one by one and took a deep breath. Then suddenly his eyes lit up.

"Well done, Bodley. That's given me an idea. I do hope Russell is right."

Bloomsbury looked about to make sure the rats had cleared off.

"We'll find out soon enough. Come along. Not a moment to lose. It's our only hope. Fancy you thinking of that. What a brainwave. Brilliant work."

Bodley hadn't a clue what he was supposed to have thought of. He couldn't recall having a brainwave before. But he was so glad to have been of service.

BRAINWAVES

Bodley followed Bloomsbury back through the maze of underground tunnels. When they resurfaced several minutes later they popped up right under the curly beards of the Winged Lions of Nimrud.

To their astonishment, the fearsome guardians of the gate had become models of good manners. They took it in turns to speak, each trying to outdo the other with excessive politeness.

"Are you sure it's my turn, Leopold?"

"Of course it is, Lionel. I dealt with the last lot."

"No, I insist. After you, Leopold."

"No, I insist. After you, Lionel."

"All right then, Leopold. If you're really sure."

At last. Lionel broke the deadlock and cleared his throat to speak.

"In the name of mighty Ashurnasirpal, who goes there?"

"It's me. Bloomsbury. I have a request. An urgent request. Matter of life and death. So there's no time for the usual palaver."

Confused, the Winged Lions fell back into the old routine, both speaking at once.

"Matter of life and death, is it? No time for the usual palaver?"

Bodley wondered what Bloomsbury had in mind. He tried in vain to listen as the bear whispered exactly what he wanted the Winged Lions to do. The twin guardians of the gate now looked even more confused. They consulted one before speaking.

"It shall be done as you request."

Seconds later, the British Museum echoed to the booming voices of the Winged Lions of Nimrud. Lionel and Leopold shouted out their lines one after the other like a well-rehearsed double-act.

"Calling all rodents!"

"Extra special deal!"

"Unique investment opportunity!"

"Only bona fide rats need apply!"

"Instant tax-free profits!"

"Unbelievable bargains!"

"Don't miss out on this one!"

"Windfall shares in Assyrian Utilities!"

"Offshore trust in Nimrud numbered account!"

"Roll up! Roll up!"

"Offer closes in five minutes!"

"Hurry! Hurry!"

"Don't miss out on this one!"

Before you could say Ashurnasirpal, a mighty torrent of excited rats descended on the Winged Lions of Nimrud. Lionel and Leopold ushered them through the gates of the city. Within two minutes every last rat in the British Museum had entered Nimrud to grab their windfall shares in Assyrian Utilities.

Bloomsbury was very satisfied with a job well done. He patted Bodley on the head. So what next? Their thoughts were interrupted by the piercing scream of a lady in distress.

"Lady Caryatid!"

Bodley rushed to her side. Bloomsbury followed a short distance behind. The lady was in great distress.

"Help! Help! The British Museum has been besieged by rats. One has had the nerve to hide here. Right under the hem of my robe, if you please! Pray take him away. Will there be no end to my suffering?"

A breathless, red-faced Russell now emerged. Lady Caryatid bestowed a warm smile on Bodley, whom she regarded as her rescuer.

"Henceforth may the Gods of Mount Olympus protect you from all perils, you brave one who has come to me in my hour of need."

Bodley looked up adoringly at Lady Caryatid. To think that in her eyes he had saved the day! Simply too wonderful for words. He was in heaven. He could have gazed at her for ever. Then, just to make his happiness perfectly complete, she addressed him in her most gracious manner.

"I can now tell you the answer to the question you wanted to ask."

But before she could speak, Bloomsbury was already ushering him away.

"You'll have to excuse us, Lady Caryatid. We've a bit of an emergency on our hands. We'll be back just as soon as we can."

That was a cruel blow. His moment of truth had been taken away. Bodley choked on his disappointment. But they didn't go far before Bloomsbury paused again for yet another spot of cool, concentrated cogitation.

"So far so good, Bodley. We've got all the rats penned up in Nimrud trying to sign on for free shares. But they'll soon rumble that little ruse. So what next? Can't you think of something else? How about another of your brainwaves?"

Bodley had never had his opinion asked for so often before. Without even thinking, he was only too pleased to offer a suggestion.

"Why not ask old Amenophis III? He has an answer for everything. I would imagine that the ancient Egyptians must have had plenty of rats."

Bloomsbury beamed approvingly.

"Capital! First rate! Why didn't I think of that? So come along. Let's get going!"

Bloomsbury, Bodley and Russell scurried along to the Egyptian Gallery. The clamour of rats screaming for free shares in Assyrian Utilities mounted in an angry crescendo. How long would the Winged Lions of Nimrud be able to hold them back?

Now the two bears and a rat arrived before Amenophis III. After Bloomsbury had explained their problem with the rats, the Pharaoh just looked on blankly in silence. They waited an eternity for him to speak. Time enough to build a great pyramid, or so it felt. At last Amenophis III spoke.

"Rats, you say? Did you say rats?"

There followed another great pyramid of a pause.

"Never had to deal personally with pest control, you know. Never dealt with anything personally of course. Just being Pharaoh was all I was ever required

137

to do. But if it's a real emergency, then I suppose an all-purpose Pharaonic curse will do the trick. Let me see if I can remember something suitable."

This sounded promising. So they waited while Amenophis III rummaged about in his dense granite brain for an ancient curse to deal with rats. Meanwhile, the rodent uproar from Nimrud increased alarmingly. Lionel and Leopold were evidently running out of excuses for the unreasonable delay in doling out the free shares in Assyrian Utilities.

Finally, the Pharaoh spoke.

"No, it's no good. Can't seem to remember any Pharaonic curses. Problem is I never had to remember anything for myself, you see. Always had someone on hand to remember everything for me."

At this, the Sakhmet Sisters intervened.

"Totally useless asking Amenophis. We'd do the job. But you don't ask lionesses to deal with rats."

It was Bodley who spoke next.

"Shame we don't have a cat or something."

With one voice, the Sakhmet Sisters exclaimed.

"Nice one, Bodley. Cool thinking. But all our cats were mummified. By order of you know who."

Amenophis III now had a flash of inspiration.

"Cats! A stroke of genius. Give that bear a pyramid. Cats! Cats!! Why didn't I think of that? I have not one but the seven fabulous Pharaonic Cats at my command. Just the job for them."

Bodley couldn't believe how many excellent ideas he was having. But then Amenophis III hesitated.

"Trouble is my cats haven't moved a muscle for more than three thousand three hundred and thirty three years. So they are probably a bit rusty."

Amenophis III fell silent, still deep in thought.

"But it might be worth a try."

Their hopes rose only to be dashed again.

"Now where did I put the Pharaonic Cats?"

Valuable time was ticking away. Already, some extremely disgruntled rodent investors had started to leave Nimrud. One sharp-eyed rat now entered the Egyptian Gallery. The three fugitives hastily hid behind the great granite arm of Amenophis III. But it was too late. They had been spotted. Now it was only a matter of time before the other rats would be summoned and they would be caught. Surely, this must be the end?

Then something magical happened. Without uttering a single word, the Pharaoh relayed a command by thought-wave to the occupants of a display case in a neighbouring gallery. There was a sound of shattering glass. Seconds later, seven of the fanciest bronze cats, each with one green and one blue eye, bowed their heads before Amenophis III. They wore golden earrings and collars studded with red gemstones. These creatures of exquisite beauty stretched their legs and arched their backs like ballet dancers limbering up. Then, after another inaudible command from the Pharaoh, they sprinted off to do his bidding.

The moment the rats got wind of the cats, they immediately lost interest in Assyrian Utilities and numbered accounts in Nimrud. They just rushed for the exit in an almighty panic. Never before has there been seen such a raging river of rodents racing for all they were worth to save their skins.

The magnificent seven Pharaonic Cats swiftly cleared the entire British Museum of every single rat, except for Russell who sheltered beneath the protective shadow of Amenophis III. Their task completed, the cats returned to pay homage to their lord and master. The Pharaoh was well pleased with them.

"Well done, fabulous felines. Take another nine lives as your reward."

Amenophis III was now well pleased with himself. He threw a sideways glance at the Sakhmet Sisters just to make sure they were too.

"Well, I sorted that one nicely, don't you reckon girls? Would you believe it? That's the first time I've ever been asked to do anything for anyone. When I was on the throne that sort of thing simply didn't happen. I had slaves for everything. I had people standing by to eat my dinner for me just in case I couldn't be bothered to eat it myself. I even had someone to yawn for me when I was too tired."

The Pharaoh paused for thought. A whole new world of exciting possibilities stretched out before him.

"Can't begin to tell you how good it feels to be useful for once. Perhaps there is some fun to be had in this place after all. Do come and see me again whenever you want anything fixed. No matter what."

Then the Pharaoh's face lit up.

"Perhaps I should start a business? All problems solved. Twenty-four hour service. Free estimates. No job too small. Never knowingly undersold. Full refund if not completely satisfied."

The Pharaoh's eager expression announced something very special.

"Listen to this! If I were to do a job for myself, I could put up a sign *By Royal Appointment*. Gosh, what a wheeze! Now what do you say to that, Sakhmet Sisters? Am I, or am I not, simply the greatest?"

The Sakhmet Sisters, unusually silent during the expulsion of the rats, now spoke all at once. They fell over one another to compliment the fantastic Pharaoh on his bold initiative and daring enterprise. Yes, they would all love to work for him in his new business.

Amenophis III felt like a real hero. He looked immensely proud and happy. He allowed his smooth granite lips to curl slowly upwards in a majestic smile of utter contentment. The two bears and a rat now took their leave. In parting, Russell made careful note of the four slinky girls with heads of lionesses. So these were the Sakhmet Sisters? They certainly had something, but still he couldn't see them as a red hot girl band. He told himself the bet with Bloomsbury was as good as won. He patted his palmtop PC, confident he would not be parting with it. But he didn't like to think what he would do with the bear's boring old research notes.

PARTING OF THE WAYS

They withdrew from the presence of the jubilant Pharaoh and made their way back up to Bloomsbury's den above the Round Reading Room. Minutes later they were sipping tea from a motley collection of chipped china cups. Bloomsbury was glad to have his paws on his own hearthrug again.

"I must say it's good to be home. Perhaps I'm a bit too set in my ways for all this rushing about. Shame about the Parchment Papers. Heaven knows how we can find them now. I fear we shall never discover what secrets they hold. But still there is plenty of work for me here. So perhaps it's really for the best the way things have worked out."

Bodley couldn't believe Bloomsbury could give up so easily on the lost manuscript, and he dreaded to think what had happened to Victor Verum.

Bloomsbury took another sip of tea.

"On the other hand, I have undeniably acquired the taste for travel. And if I stay here, how will I ever get to see *The Great Bear* in Oxford?"

Bodley didn't know what to say to this. He blushed at the false information he had put in Bloomsbury's mind. But this wasn't the moment to tell him the truth. To avoid his eyes he walked over to the gap in the bookshelf and peered through. The Round Reading Room had just opened its doors. The first readers were collecting their books for another day's hard labour. Directly below him, Bodley spotted the colourful bag belonging to Professor Parchment. It was unmistakable. His heart leapt with joy. The manuscript might be inside? Victor Verum too? If so, then they could all escape to Oxford. In a frenzy of excitement Bodley turned to his friends.

"He's here! Parchment is here! He must be here. His bag is on the desk. Come quickly, not a moment to lose! Let's go! Let's go!"

Bloomsbury took one more sip from his cup of tea and followed them down to the Round Reading Room. The moment they reached the place where Parchment's bag was lying, Bodley dived inside. But he found no trace of the manuscript, nor of Victor Verum. Sadly, he joined Bloomsbury and Russell waiting on the desktop behind a small pile of books.

"I'm afraid the manuscript isn't there. But I suppose the Prof might be carrying it."

That hope didn't last for very long. They now saw Professor Parchment returning to his place in the Round Reading Room. He dragged himself along, as if suffering from a great heaviness of heart. He had aged years in a single night. He slumped onto his chair, holding his head in his hands.

"My life's work snatched away. It's the end of the world. What am I to do?"

So the manuscript had indeed been stolen along with dear Victor Verum inside it. Bodley could contain himself no longer. Between gulps and sobs, he unburdened his feelings to Bloomsbury and Russell.

"He's not here! Poor Victor. Such a dear fellow. Trapped in the manuscript. Wrapped in a parcel. Stolen by a thief. Vanished. Gone forever."

None of this made any sense to Bloomsbury.

"What is the matter with you, Bodley? It's the second time you've mentioned this Victor. You must now tell me exactly who he is and what he has to do with Professor Parchment's lost manuscript. This time, I don't want to hear any more of those tall stories that you make up on the spur of the moment."

Bodley watched every gesture on Bloomsbury's face as he told him the truth about Victor Verum, bookworm in residence at the Bodleian Library, now certainly imprisoned in the stolen manuscript. Bloomsbury became most upset on learning that such a dangerous creature had entered his inner sanctum. He prayed his own research notes hadn't been eaten.

"You see, Bodley. Bookworms and bears don't mix. We are definitely at odds with one another. What we create, they destroy."

"Victor isn't like that. He only eats the useless stuff. He told me so himself."

Bloomsbury eyed Bodley like a hopeless case.

"He would say that, wouldn't he? You should be more concerned about the missing manuscript than a lost bookworm. What a catastrophe! Even if your precious Victor Verum is still inside the parcel, that only makes matters worse. At this very moment he is probably making a meal of it. Just imagine how poor Professor Parchment must feel. Think of his loss. But what did he mean about the end of the world? There really must be something of global importance in those papers. I do wish we could do something."

Bloomsbury cogitated very hard. But nothing seemed to come of it.

"What do you think, Russell?"

The rat had a more practical view of things.

"None of this would have happened if Professor Parchment had made a back-up copy on disk."

"Back-up copy on disk? What on earth is that?"

"Never mind, Bloomers. No use crying over spilt milk. Or, as we rats say, you can't ungrate the cheese."

Russell's mood changed. He fancied a treasure hunt as much as anyone and now he had a hunch about the Parchment Papers. He asked about the exact circumstances when and where the manuscript had been stolen. His listened attentively to Bodley's garbled account of the thief snatching the bag and turning out its contents on the ground just before the two bears fell down the hole and landed in the tunnel where they met Russell. He was on the point of saying something. But he kept quiet. Russell's hunch would be more than a bit dangerous to check out. If his suspicions were correct, then the outlook both for the Parchment Papers and for Victor Verum was far worse than the two bears could possibly imagine.

In any case, there was no time to pursue his speculation. A lady at the next desk had spotted Russell, only half hidden behind a pile of books.

She let out a violent yell.

"Aaaagh!!! There's a rat on that man's desk! Will someone call pest control? For heaven's sake!!!"

Russell darted into the bag. Pest control? He didn't like the sound of that. Bloomsbury and Bodley scrambled in after him.

"Aaaagh!!! Aaaagh!!!"

The lady's hysterical screams echoed in the great dome of the Round Reading Room. Professor Parchment, unaware of the cause of her alarm, asked her kindly to restrain herself. This only provoked another outburst of hysteria. The lady screamed again and ran off for help. Moments later, a uniformed British Museum warden came over to investigate. The sobbing lady followed in his wake.

Trembling inside the bag, the two bears listened gravely to Russell.

"Always the same when someone sees a rat. They won't rest until they've caught me."

Bloomsbury's solid faith in cool, concentrated cogitation was shaken. Things were moving too fast. He couldn't think of a way for Russell to save his skin.

"You must look after yourself, Russell. Don't worry about us."

Russell addressed them in grave tones.

"Listen carefully, my friends. The game is up, at least for me. If I don't make a run for it now they'll roast my whiskers and worse. But you must stay here in the bag and escape with Professor Parchment to Oxford. The rats won't think of looking for you there."

The two bears promised to do as he said. Only now did they fully realise just how very fond they had become of Russell in such a short time. The prospect of losing him filled them with despair.

"Just stay put, and you'll be OK. We've come through a few scrapes. There may be many more to come. But for now, it's farewell, old pals."

The museum warden now prodded Professor Parchment in the back.

"Lady here says you're harbouring a rat in that there bag, sir."

The official looked like he meant business.

"So just hand it over. Nice and easy now. No sudden movements and no funny tricks."

The man's rough hand reached out to grab the bag. At that precise moment, Russell took a huge leap into space. He shot up like a cork from a champagne bottle. For a split second he hung high in the air, eyeball to eyeball with the BM warden whose jaw dropped open like a trapdoor in utter amazement. The tearful lady, now confronted by a flying rat, suffered yet another fit of hysterical screaming.

"Aaaagh!!! Aaaagh!!!"

Russell poked out his tongue at her.

"Call pest control if you want! But they'll have to catch me first!"

On his way down to earth, Russell saw the British Museum cat lying in wait. For good measure, he cocked a snook at it too. The instant his paws touched the ground, Russell went into top gear. Before you could say *rattus rattus* or *rattus norwegicus*, he had whizzed out of the Round Reading Room.

Now Bodley also took his leave.

"Forgive me, Bloomsbury. But I can't stay here. Not while Russell is in such danger. You go to Oxford with Parchment. I'll know where to find you. Now I must go and help him. Goodbye."

There was no way Bloomsbury could hold him back. Everything was happening ten times faster than he could deal with. He was so stunned by Bodley's departure he couldn't speak. Anyway, it was too late for words. He watched his young friend race after the rat. Now he was on his own.

Russell sprinted down the steps of the British Museum. Two fat pigeons were pecking grumpily at some crumbs. They saw a tiny blur of fur followed by a larger one, which they immediately recognised as a cat. They didn't see Bodley following on behind.

"Stone the bloomin' crows, Fred!"

"A flamin' pussycat, Joe!"

"Let's beat it, Fred!"

"On yer bike, Joe!"

Fred and Joe made frantic efforts to take off. Luckily for them the British Museum cat was so intent on catching Russell it didn't spot the two pigeons struggling to get airborne. After much huffing and puffing, they flew up to the branch of a plane tree in the courtyard. From this vantage-point, they watched Russell speed down the road and take a sharp left into Coptic Street, with the BM cat in hottest pursuit.

"Blimey, that was a close shave, Joe."

"I'm right out of breath, Fred."

"Feel a bit dizzy myself, Joe."

"Me old ticker needs a rest, Fred."

"Gotta fag on yer, Joe?"

Meanwhile, excitement was running high in the Round Reading Room. After Russell's hasty departure, attention now fell on an acutely embarrassed Professor Parchment. He tried to explain he was not responsible for the rat. No really, he had definitely not smuggled it in. It was nothing to do with him. But his voice lacked conviction. He knew they didn't believe him. Feeling lower than ever, he took up his bag and left.

He wondered if he could ever again show his face in these sacred halls of scholarship. Once outside, he wandered about the neighbourhood, his sad eyes trailing on the pavements in the vain hope he would find his missing manuscript. By late afternoon, he lost heart altogether and caught the bus back to Oxford.

Still concealed inside the professor's bag, and not knowing what else he should do, Bloomsbury thoughts were only for his friends.

"Brave, big-hearted Russell. So much heroism in a small rodent. Two bears protected by a mere slip of a rat, and dear Bodley, poor lad. Why didn't I stop him? What will become of him out there all alone on the streets of London? Then there's Parchment's stolen manuscript and the end of the world in prospect. All too much to take in at once. Far too much."

In this sorry state, Bloomsbury fell asleep. He missed a glorious sunset as the bus reached the crest of the Chiltern Hills. He awoke briefly when he was dropped with a great bump on Professor Parchment's springy sofa. Then he slept again. He had arrived safe and sound in Oxford, but his dreams were full of dread and anxiety for Bodley and Russell.

Bodley's situation was desperate indeed. He couldn't possibly keep up with the speedy Russell hotly pursued by the BM cat. Very soon he was left far behind and utterly lost. He drifted aimlessly about the streets hoping he would pick up the trail. Suddenly his courage deserted him. He wished he had no courage at all rather than just a bit. That way he would have played it safe and avoided getting into hot water. He hadn't a clue what to do. His action had been pointless. He wasn't able to help anyone, and there was no one to help him. Why hadn't he listened to Russell and stayed with Bloomsbury? Not knowing what else to do, he crept inside an empty cardboard box in a doorway. Why hadn't he listened to Belinda and stuck to the Prof? Whatever would become of him now?

RAT ON THE RUN

He had got off to a flying start, but Russell couldn't shake off the BM cat. Dart and dodge as he might in the maze of streets, his pursuer was able to follow his every move. Every time he looked over his shoulder and thought he was clean away, he saw the cat still on his trail. Clearly, this pussycat was no one's fool.

Exhausted as he was, Russell found strength to whiz across the busy main road of Southampton Row risking his neck right under the wheels of the traffic. Luck was on his side. He narrowly avoided being run over. Then he made the sharpest of turns down a narrow alley. He was now on his last legs. He could barely walk, let alone run much further. The BM cat, sensing victory at last, tracked him step for step. On entering Queen Square, Russell still had a short lead. But the cat was closing in on him.

Then, disaster struck. All of a sudden he had to step on the brakes to avoid a full frontal collision with the menacing muzzle of Reginald Rottweiler. The dog bared its teeth, seeing a chance to settle old scores. At this critical point, Russell's quick rodent intelligence came to his rescue.

"Afternoon, Reggie. Can't stop now, old chap. Big pussycat on the way over. Reckons it can sort you out. Been boasting to everyone. What are you going to do about it? Look, here he comes now."

Reginald Rottweiler gave out a deadly growl as the BM cat bowled blithely into Queen Square. In a split second of horror the hunter realised it was now the hunted. The cat stopped in its tracks, arched its back and almost shed its fur coat in a lightning about turn. It looked desperately for the nearest refuge. Seeing no tree tall enough for safety, it scrambled up the wall of St George the Martyr. The terrified animal didn't stop climbing until it had reached the very top of the church spire where it clung on to the weathercock for dear life. Far below, the angry dog howled and growled in a great lather of furious barking.

Russell jumped for joy. He was safe. But his triumph was short lived. In the middle of his victory dance he lost his footing. As he stumbled about trying to regain his balance, the ground seemed to give way beneath him. Before he knew it he was falling down a deep hole. In desperation he stuck out a paw. By good fortune it latched on to something solid. Russell found he was grasping an iron bar. He dangled in space until his paws located another iron bar directly beneath him. He was clutching the rungs of a ladder.

As Russell looked into the dark depths he remembered how Bodley and Bloomsbury had fallen down just such a hole. He wondered whether this could be the same one. Perched precariously on the ladder, he fished out his palmtop PC to check his position. He quickly calculated he was right above the very spot on the Piccadilly Line where he had discovered the two bears. Then he recalled his hunch just a moment ago in the Round Reading Room.

He had noticed something at the time when he had found Bloomsbury and Bodley. What was it he had asked the two bears just before they set off for the Rat Race? Something about luggage, wasn't it? Yes, that was it! Did they have any luggage? Why would he have asked that? Because he had spotted something lying on the ground behind them in the dark. Something he must have assumed belonged to them. But then they'd said they hadn't brought any luggage with them. So what had he seen? Could that have been the package containing the Parchment Papers? Perhaps it had fallen down the hole just before them?

There was only one way to find out. Russell clung to the ladder weighing up the risks of being caught by his fellow rats. Then he thought of Bodley's dear friend the bookworm Victor Verum trapped in the package. After that, Russell decided he must go straight down and investigate. He had no choice.

As he descended the ladder, Russell heard the familiar rumble of trains on the Piccadilly Line far below. He hoped there wouldn't be any rat sentries posted. If there were a rodent reception committee, then he would stand no chance. Suppressing these fears, he continued his dangerous descent into the gloomy entrails of the London Underground.

He finally reached the bottom of the iron ladder which curved away around the side of the tunnel and brought him down onto the railway tracks. Yes, this was the spot where he had met up with the two bears. So where was the thing he had mistaken for their luggage? He sniffed about in the dark. He wondered if he had after all remembered correctly. But his hunch soon proved right. After several minutes Russell located the brown paper package tied up with string. It lay on the ground half hidden under the live rail.

He quickly untied the string and felt inside. Yes, this must be what all the fuss was about. This loose bundle of papers could only be Professor Parchment's missing manuscript. Russell was just on the point of wrapping it up again when he noticed two big green eyes blinking at him like a pair of traffic lights on go. A pathetic voice addressed him.

"*Servitum vostrum* surrenders. I'll come without a struggle. Please don't hurt me!"

Russell hissed at Victor Verum to be quiet.

"Keep schtumm, Vic old sport. We've got to get out of here and fast."

Russell's sharp hearing had picked up the sound of rat footsteps out there not far away in the dark tunnel. It dawned on him the shining green eyes of the bookworm must surely be proclaiming their presence as clearly as a neon advertisement.

Russell concealed Victor Verum in his waistcoat pocket, retied the Parchment Papers and hitched the packet on his back with the length of string. The manuscript weighed more than he did. All this took much longer than he reckoned. By the time Russell located the ladder and crept a few rungs around the curved wall and up towards the roof of the tunnel the light of a rodent patrol was approaching fast from the direction of Holborn. Just a bit further and he would be safely concealed in the ventilation shaft. But with the heavy package on his back this was no easy matter. One false move and he would come tumbling down.

Russell was still not completely out of sight when the rodent patrol arrived on the scene and halted. Two rats stood right underneath him. All one of them had to do was look up and Russell would be discovered. What had caught their attention and caused them to stop? Russell held his breath and prayed he hadn't left any tell-tale sign that would give the game away.

Luckily, the two rats had other things on their mind. They smoked a cigarette while they chatted.

"Don't see much point patrolling this beat."

"Nor me neither. Russell's hardly likely to come back to his old patch."

"Too bloomin' obvious by half."

"Our Russell's far too smart for that."

"Still, you never know. We might strike lucky."

"Then we'll get our paws on all that big reward that's up for grabs."

"Not to mention the gruesome punishment they've got lined up for Russell."

"Yeah, that'll be fun. Well worth waiting for."

Russell froze. The package with the Parchment Papers was heavy. The string cut into his skin. Any moment now he might lose his grip and drop into their arms like a plucked turkey. Just when he could bear it no longer the two flashlights pointed in the direction of Russell Square and slowly moved off down the tunnel.

"So we'd better keep our eyes peeled."

Their voices faded as they walked away. Russell began the long, hard climb up the ladder. After a few rungs, he paused to listen once more. Sure enough, he heard the muffled scratch and squeal of another rat patrol passing the very spot where he had been standing just a moment ago. It had been a close run thing. He didn't like to imagine that *gruesome punishment* his fellow rats had in store for him.

The long climb back to street level was painfully slow, every single inch a huge effort. Russell struggled on bravely up the iron ladder, rung after rung. All the time the weight of the manuscript on his back threatened to drag him down. His heart sounded like a drum. His head went dizzy. He felt he was going to faint. His grip on the ladder loosened.

He was about to fall back into the dark abyss when an unseen hand reached out from above to grab him and hold him fast. Was he being captured? It could make no difference. His strength was finished. He had no choice but to allow himself to be hauled up the last long stretch. He wouldn't have managed on his own. Finally, he saw a glimmer of daylight above him. Only then did he catch sight of his rescuer.

Russell found himself looking into a very familiar face. He couldn't believe his eyes.

"Bodley! What are you doing here? Shouldn't you be in Oxford? That was the plan, wasn't it?"

"Plans can change. I'll tell you why later. Let's get you back on solid ground first."

Slowly but surely Bodley dragged Russell out of the dark hole. When they reached the top at last, he removed the heavy packet from his back. They both fell exhausted behind a bush. Russell started to speak the moment he caught his breath.

"You really saved my skin, Bodley."

"Oh, it was nothing."

Russell permitted himself a brief smile.

"Or should I say our skins?"

Russell inserted a paw in his waistcoat pocket. When he withdrew it, there – to Bodley's great delight – was Victor Verum beaming from ear to ear.

"Victor, my dear fellow. I've been so worried. You've no idea."

"*Servitum vostrum* is eternally in your debt, my dear Bodley. Also to the brave stranger who came to the rescue in my darkest hour."

Victor Verum looked gratefully at Russell.

"Best save the speech of thanks for later, Victor. We're not out of the woods. Not by a long chalk."

So a rat, a bear and a bookworm lay low and peered warily out of the bush where they had taken refuge. Queen Square, scene of Russell's encounter with Reginald Rottweiler, was now filled with a crowd of people all looking up at the spire of St George the Martyr. Those who hadn't witnessed the earlier events couldn't understand why the BM cat was hanging on for all it was worth to the lofty perch normally reserved for the exclusive use of the golden weathercock.

Russell overheard someone say the London Fire Brigade had been called out. He smiled contentedly. That could only mean one thing. As soon as the BM cat had been rescued it would be taken away for a full check-up on a vet's couch. Then it would spend the night under close medical observation while everyone made an enormous fuss of it. People were like that about cats. Meanwhile, the British Museum would be catless and as safe as houses for Russell. But how to get there unnoticed by his rat enemies?

Bodley had been making his own situation analysis. As far as he could see, the top priority was also to get back to the British Museum. He knew it wouldn't be easy carrying the heavy package of the Parchment Papers. Some sort of transport was needed. Suddenly, he had yet another idea.

"See that chap over there, Russell? The one with the suitcase on wheels. Let's hitch a ride with him."

The chap in question was an elderly Japanese tourist. He had stopped to find out why everyone was so fascinated by the church. Poor eyesight prevented him from seeing the BM cat hanging from the weathercock. So he concluded that Londoners must be extremely interested in the spires of old churches. He pointed his camcorder to record the curious scene to show his friends back home in Tokyo.

They crept out from their hiding place, dragging the Parchment Papers behind them. They scrambled onto the suitcase while the Japanese tourist had his back turned, still trying to see what all the fuss was about. In this exposed position they waited. Then, after a minute or two, the suitcase responded to a tug on its lead as if it were a dog being taken out for a walk. It was a wobbly ride. As luck had it, Bodley's inspired guess proved correct and the Japanese tourist took them straight to the British Museum.

He paused and took out his camcorder once again. This was their chance to jump ship. Russell and Bodley clambered down smartly from the suitcase carrying the Parchment Papers between them. They slipped furtively through the railings and scampered across the forecourt. It didn't take Bodley long to locate the secret trapdoor, through which they had followed Bloomsbury earlier that day. Quick as a flash, they disappeared from view. This time no one spotted them. The gamble had paid off.

Several minutes later, they surfaced through an air vent and popped up right under the curly beards of the fearsome Winged Lions of Nimrud.

"Do you see what I see, Lionel?"

"What's that, Leopold?"

159

"It's one of those bears, Lionel."

"There's a rat too, Leopold."

"A rat, Lionel? How very nasty!"

"Should we not advise Ashurnasirpal, Leopold?"

"Or perhaps Amenophis III, Lionel?"

"Then he could get those Pharaonic Cats to take care of the rodent, Leopold."

"Exactly, Lionel. Assuming the cats haven't gone back to sleep."

"That would be just typical of those Egyptians, Leopold."

They left the Winged Lions of Nimrud to their deliberations. Russell led the way round the corner to where Lady Caryatid lived. But the moment she saw the rat, she uttered a piercing scream.

"Oh ye Gods of Mount Olympus! That rat again! Save me!! Help!!!"

Victor Verum now emerged from Russell's waistcoat pocket to reassure Lady Caryatid with a few well-chosen words in ancient Greek to the effect that Russell was a gallant gentleman rat who meant her no harm. Lady Caryatid was most impressed by Victor Verum's elegant turn of phrase.

"At last, someone who speaks the language of the Gods! Welcome strangers, and pray tell me how Lady Caryatid can be of service."

Then Lady Caryatid noticed Bodley modestly bringing up the rear. She beckoned him to approach.

"You may now redeem the pledge I made you."

Bodley didn't know what to say.

"The pledge?"

"I promised to tell you what you want to know."

Still he did not speak.

"It's about who you are, isn't it?"

Suddenly, Bodley was strangely reluctant to find out who he really was. It seemed just fine being Bodley, and doing what he was doing was also just fine or even better. On top of that, there were much more pressing matters to sort out than to discover who he had been in a former life.

"Thank you, Lady Caryatid, I do appreciate the kind offer. But may I ask you to hold my secret in your care for later? There are urgent things that need seeing to right away. Matters of life and death."

Lady Caryatid eyed him with interest.

"That is a most unusual decision. Knowledge of that sort is not given lightly. Most mortals are desperate to possess it."

Lady Caryatid had such a serious look. Bodley thought he had made an awful mistake. But then her eyes softened into a smile.

"However, on reflection, I think you have made a wise choice. In fact, you show wisdom and maturity beyond your years. Knowing who you are should wait on the correct moment for its revelation. Besides, it will have far more worth if you find out for yourself. Meanwhile, not knowing who you are, may be better for the task you have to accomplish."

Bodley hadn't figured it out quite like that. It all sounded a bit too grand and far too much of a riddle.

But he could see roughly what she meant. He might not yet have a clue who he was and he still faced all sorts of dangers, but he was making good friends, having adventures and learning things that kept on surprising him. Most important of all was the fact that Lady Caryatid had praised him so generously. So he must be doing something right.

Bodley was about to round things off nicely with a polite phrase. But the words froze in his mouth. By some ancient Egyptian magic, the Pharaonic Cats had crept up completely unheard and unseen. They had materialised out of thin air. There they were standing around in a threatening circle. Now they bared their fangs. What had upset them? Russell was in no doubt.

"It must be me they're after."

Russell was right. For had not Amenophis III commanded the Pharaonic Cats to dispose of all rats in the British Museum? So who was this one impudent rodent who dared to defy them! The beautiful animals extended their sharp claws and hissed at Russell. They had him at their mercy.

Victor Verum now came unexpectedly to the rescue. He beamed his big green eyes on each of the seven cats in turn. They seemed mesmerised by the tiny worm. Now Bodley again seized the initiative.

"I know you are only obeying orders, fantastic felines. But this particular rat stands under the Pharaoh's special protection. So I think you had better take him unharmed straight to Amenophis III."

The Pharaonic Cats consulted one another through flashing eye signals of blue and green. Then they escorted their prisoners away. How Bodley wished Bloomsbury was there to explain matters properly. Would Amenophis III take kindly to him after the hard time he had given him over the *who am I?* question. He hoped the Pharaoh would be merciful.

OUT ON THE TOWN

Closely guarded by the Pharaonic Cats, Bodley, Russell and Victor Verum entered the Egyptian Gallery to encounter an amazing scene. Amenophis III was eagerly watching the feverish activity of the four Sakhmet Sisters. The girls knelt before him busy with brushes and paint pots scattered all over the floor. Russell examined them with particular interest. They still didn't look as if they had the makings of a hit girl band, and if they were going to work full time painting posters there was no way they would be anything like hot property on the music scene by the end of the week. He reflected grimly that at least his bet with Bloomsbury was safe, even if he personally wasn't.

The Sakhmet Sisters were totally engrossed in putting the finishing touches to a large banner, which announced in brightly coloured letters:

AMENOPHIS ENTERPRISES. BY ROYAL APPOINTMENT. ALL PROBLEMS SORTED: BIG, SMALL AND MEDIUM. REASONABLE RATES. BRAINSTORMING INCLUDED. APPLY WITHIN. NEVER KNOWINGLY UNDERSOLD.

The Pharaoh now noticed Russell whom the cats nudged forward for inspection.

"I say, girls. look what the Pharaonic Cats have brought in. We haven't even put up the sign and here's our first customer!. I knew this was a smart move. Keep at it sisters. Time is money, you know."

With a flick of the eyes, Amenophis III dismissed the cats. He would have liked a more substantial client to launch his business. Furthermore, he wasn't too sure how to address a lowly rat. But business was business.

"So what's the problem, minuscule rodent? No, let's skip that. It'll save time if I get cracking with the brainstorming right away. So let's cut to the chase and get my head round the creative bit. Thinking the unthinkable. Blue sky ideas. Outside the box. Platform 9¾. That kind of stuff. Won't take a moment. Grab a pew. The girls will fix you a coffee."

Amenophis III rolled his big eyes to the heavens and began storming his great granite brain for an answer to Russell's problem, whatever it was. The Sakhmet Sisters couldn't hold back their laughter.

"Silly old Amenophis! Fancy trying to solve the problem before asking what it is! He'll never get anywhere. But it's no use telling him."

Amenophis III continued his solo brainstorming, while the savvy Sakhmet Sisters quizzed Russell and quickly sussed what needed to be done. Namely, they had to get him, Bodley and Victor Verum along with the Parchment Papers to Oxford as fast as possible. It was just so blindingly obvious.

They waited impatiently for Amenophis III to come to the same conclusion. Several minutes passed without any response. He seemed to have stopped breathing. So they waited some more, but still with no result. Eventually, one of the Sakhmet Sisters climbed up on the shoulders of another and whispered something into the Pharaoh's right ear. Seconds later, Amenophis III opened his eyes.

"OK, team. Brainstorming over. The oracle has spoken. We have a result. Russell & Co must take the next bus to Oxford. Problem sorted. Invoice in the post. Happy client. Bring on the next!"

Amenophis III appeared none too clear about the advice he had given. For he now turned to the Sakhmet Sisters for an explanation.

"What is a bus, by the way, girls?"

The giggling Sakhmet Sisters told the Pharaoh that in his capacity as President and Chairman of Amenophis Enterprises he need not bother himself with tiny details like that. They would take care of everything and personally escort Russell, Bodley and Victor Verum to this bus thing.

"Better take the Pharaonic Cats, girls."

As it happened, this turned out to be a very sensible suggestion.

"Don't stay out too late!"

With that Amenophis III sank back into his habitual state of majestic repose, clearly exhausted by all his mental exertions.

The Sakhmet Sisters waited until it was very late before venturing forth. It was well after midnight when a small procession emerged from the British Museum. Three Pharaonic Cats walked on ahead, while another three brought up the rear. Safely placed between them, Bodley and Russell rode in majestic style on the back of the seventh Pharaonic Cat with Victor Verum perched on the Parchment Papers. Two of the stunning Sakhmet Sisters flanked them on either side. They had made themselves up to look even more gorgeous than ever. The assembled company formed the most exotic and sensational parade ever to have graced the streets of London. They looked like the courtly nobles of a rich oriental sheikh or maharajah on a state visit.

According to the information Russell had downloaded, their destination was Trafalgar Square, where the night bus to Oxford stopped to pick up passengers every hour throughout the night. But the Sakhmet Sisters, wildly excited by the glitz and glamour of all the fashion shops and music stores, couldn't resist making a huge detour along Oxford Street. This was by far the best thing they had seen since the good old days back in Thebes when they had bought up just about everything in the exotic bazaars.

"Just look at all the bright lights, girls!"

"What do you say to all that classy clobber?"

"Those platform shoes look well wicked."

"Our kind of town, or what?"

Amid such happy chatter, the Sakhmet Sisters turned down Regent Street, attracted by yet more shops curving away in the distance. They stopped in awe at Piccadilly Circus, dazzled by the neon ads behind the Eros Fountain. Even Russell, who knew London so well he reckoned nothing could surprise him, was utterly entranced. Never had his hometown appeared to him so mind-bogglingly magnificent as it did that night. He couldn't decide which one of the four slinky

Egyptian girls he liked the most. They strutted like supermodels down a catwalk. Something in the way they moved, he just couldn't keep his eyes off them. Now they certainly looked like a seriously hot number, and if it turned out they could sing, then his bet with Bloomsbury was as good as lost..

Bodley and Victor Verum, newcomers to the big city, stared in all directions at once lapping up every detail. The bookworm's wide luminous green eyes grew ever brighter and larger, adding their own shining wonderment to the magic of the scene.

They continued to Leicester Square, empty but for a few youngsters who had been out on the town and were now slowly heading home. The streetwise kids figured the Pharaonic Cats and the Sakhmet Sisters to be a lavish publicity stunt promoting yet another new show. They scarcely gave them a second glance.

Russell was glad hardly anyone was about. They had almost reached their goal. The last thing he wanted was to attract unwelcome attention from a rat patrol. The group now headed south down Charing Cross Road towards Trafalgar Square, ever closer to the bus that would take the three fugitives and their precious package to the safety of Oxford.

No sooner had the Sakhmet Sisters caught sight of the four mighty lions guarding Nelson's Column than they hurried forward.

"Just take a look at these guys."

"There's one for each of us."

"Big brutes or what?"

"Aren't they gorgeous?"

The Sakhmet Sisters climbed all over the lions while the Pharaonic Cats leapt up onto the plinth and prowled around. Russell looked about apprehensively. His whiskers began to twitch nervously. Something bad was about to happen. He didn't have to wait long to find out what.

A posse of drunken rats burst noisily into Trafalgar Square from St Martins Lane. Still perched on the back of a Pharaonic Cat, Russell was dangerously exposed to view. There was nowhere to hide. He was spotted straight away by one of the rats.

"Look! That's Russell up there! Come on, let's nail the treacherous bastard!"

SAKHMET SISTERS ON A HIGH

A handful of rats rushed forward to take Russell. They were immediately joined by more and then still more rats. Before long, Trafalgar Square was wall to wall with angry, agitated rodents. Luckily, the stone plinth on which Russell stood was too high for them to climb, and the fearsome sight of the seven Pharaonic Cats skulking about kept them at bay. Russell, unable to conceal himself, had to face the aggressive taunts of the raucous rats in the first few rows.

"You'll have to come down sooner or later, Russell. Then we'll get you."

"We'll be right here waiting for you!"

At this one of the rats started singing.

"Why are we waiting? Why are we waiting?"

Then they all joined in. But when they were finished singing, things took a more sinister tone.

"Now let's have a song from you."

"Yeah, a song. That's right, Russell!"

"First we'll hear you sing!"

"Then we'll make you sing!"

Not that he particularly wanted to sing in his present predicament. But anything to buy time would help. So with shaking voice, Russell sang his song to the melody of *A Slow Boat to China:*

"I'm going to take you
Down the info super-highway
And out into cyberspace ..."

The rats drowned his nervous efforts with a huge chorus of boos and jeers. At this moment, Russell saw the night bus to Oxford pull away from the stop. Now he would have to spin things out for another hour.

"Can't you do better than that, Russell?"

"Don't you know any other songs?"

"Something about the Global Index, perhaps?"

"Or how's about the teddy bear's picnic?"

Russell was getting desperate. He racked his brains for something to sing. He could think of nothing except for the little ditty he had started to compose back there in the tunnel. He decided to give it a try. He cleared his throat and began to sing.

"No need to know anything
Except when I need to know it.
No need to go anywhere,
Except when I need to go it."

But this only made matters worse.

"Don't even think about going anywhere!"

"You ain't going nowhere, Russell!!"

Exhausted, terrified, breathless – and for once in his life clueless as well – Russell turned to Bodley. Without hesitation, Bodley whispered something to the Sakhmet Sisters. The quick-witted girls immediately twigged what he wanted them to do. Seconds later they started humming along like a backing group to give Russell some support while he caught his breath.

At first, this brought more boos and jeers but the Sakhmet Sisters were not intimidated by the seething mass of irate rodents. In fact, the crowd reminded them so vividly of their riotous all-night mega-gigs on the banks of the Nile when they regularly played to thousands and thousands of screaming fans who weren't that easy to please. They'd always ended up with them all eating out of their hands easy as pie.

"Haven't seen an audience like this for ages."

"Shall we give them one of our songs?"

"Reckon we should?"

"Fancy our chances of a comeback?"

"Must be worth a go."

"Come on then, sisters!"

"Let's go for it!"

"Take five, Russell."

"You can leave this little lot to us."

Even before they had sung their first note, it was obvious they were going to be huge. Serious big-time. Cosmic. Awesome. Orbital. The Sakhmet Sisters had the aura of stardom about them. Now their moment had come. It was as if they had but a single night to catch up on the three thousand three hundred and thirty three years that had elapsed since their last concert had resounded over the moonlit waters of the Nile. The years rolled back in the twinkling of an eye as the girls began to sing. Wow!

With an easy familiarity, they settled smoothly into the groove as they crooned their way through the old repertoire. Their music had an enchanting oriental lilt to it, which soon had the entire multitude of rats under its spell. The bewitching lyrics befuddled their brains like magic spells, making them forget everything but the wonderful music filling their heads.

Russell, who had seen a girl band or two in his time, was in transports of delight. Sheer magic. How could stuffy old Bloomsbury possibly have predicted such a musical sensation? Perhaps there was a lot more to bears than he had assumed? At any rate, he knew he had lost his bet. No contest. But he couldn't care less. This was a moment to die for. He was blithely happy and he completely forgot the danger he was in.

Time stopped while the Sakhmet Sisters sang on and on. A mood of peace descended. It was as if all the troubles of the world were carried away on the sweet waves of their voices. The way they shimmied and wiggled up and down so seductively was mesmerising. Their songs entered the very flesh and bones of the audience. The whole crowd of rats moved helplessly to the beat, enslaved by the rhythm. Trafalgar Square swayed to and fro like a field of flowers blowing in the wind, every single rat spinning like a whirling dervish.

If there could ever be a moment to cry out for time to stop and say enough is enough, this is as good as it gets, then this was it. The Sakhmet Sisters were ablaze with glory, riding the crest of an all-time high.

"Just like the old days."

"Better."

"Never seen anything like it."

"Why haven't we played to rats before?"

"You've got to hand it to these rodents."

"Sure know how to rave."

Indeed, they did. The rats were released from all, care, concern and anger about the Global Index. They let themselves go with total abandon. They held nothing back as they danced to the beat. They forgot even their pursuit of the rogue rodent Russell who had been the cause of all their woes.

Steadily the Sakhmet Sisters upped the tempo. They whipped the rats into a seething mass of stomping and bopping. The general hubbub shook Trafalgar Square and even threatened to topple Lord Nelson off the top of his column. Two snoozing pigeons, unsteadily perched on the one-eyed admiral's hat, were woken by the great din down below.

"What's all this, Fred?"

"Should be a law against it, Joe!"

"Just like bloomin' Benidorm, innit?"

"Oi, you lot. Put a sock in it, for gawd's sake!"

But in spite of themselves, the two grumpy pigeons were also hopping to the beat, although each pretended he was just shuffling about to keep warm.

Now the next night bus to Oxford roared into Trafalgar Square and pulled up at the stop. Bodley was almost sorry to see it. He wanted this night to last for ever. But there was Russell to think about. So he passed the word to the Sakhmet Sisters who then whispered a command to the Pharaonic Cats.

Six of the seven felines instantly went into action. As if dividing a flock of sheep, they cleared a path through the raving rats. It didn't take Russell a moment to grasp the plan. Making sure Victor Verum was safely tucked away in his waistcoat pocket and taking hold of the Parchment Papers, he reached out to grab the jewel-encrusted collar of the one remaining Pharaonic Cat. The magnificent animal obligingly lowered its head and Russell swung himself up to join Bodley who was already perched on its supple back.

It was now or never. The Pharaonic Cat leapt from the plinth of Nelson's Column and raced down the open passage between the serried ranks of raving rodents kept clear by the constant prowling of the other six cats. Russell rode past right under the very noses of his fellow rats who would surely have lynched him if they had had the chance. But so utterly entranced were they by the sublime singing of the Sakhmet Sisters they didn't even notice the traitor Russell and his bear accomplice make their amazing getaway.

The Pharaonic Cat streaked across the road with Russell and Bodley clinging on for all they were worth. Just as it reached the bus it stopped dead in its tracks and propelled them on board with a deft flick of its neck. There was no time for thank you or farewell. No sooner had they picked themselves up and made sure they had both Victor Verum and the Parchment Papers still with them, than the bus closed its doors and set off for Oxford. All too soon the divine music of the Sakhmet Sisters became a faint echo. Like a wonderful dream fading away. They couldn't help but cry with pain when eventually they could hear it no more.

Meanwhile, back in Trafalgar Square, the Sakhmet Sisters kept the show rolling until the first red streaks of dawn came spilling along the Strand. The raving rats were still going strong when the gallant girl singers signed off with their own ancient Egyptian lullaby Sunrise on the Nile.

> *"You can bongo on the Congo,*
> *Sip cocoa on the Limpopo.*
> *Or take it nice and easy*
> *On the shores of the Zambezi.*
> *But nothing beats the smile*
> *Of a sunrise on the Nile."*

This gentle melody brought the rats gently down to earth. No longer driven by the frenzy of the music, the groovy rodents unwound like clockwork toys, until at last they all collapsed one by one in a great heap and fell asleep. Trafalgar Square was completely covered with their furry snoozing bodies.

Only then did the Sakhmet Sisters call it a day and softly steal away. The sun was already up as they got back to the British Museum. They tiptoed breathlessly to their place in the Egyptian Gallery, not caring if Amenophis III would be monumentally angry to discover they had been out all night. But the Pharaoh didn't so much as bat a granite eyelid. The Pharaonic Cats padded away purring contentedly. For them too it had been just like old times. No, even better. They hadn't had such fun for ages.

HOME SWEET HOME

Even as Russell, Bodley and Victor Verum sped towards Oxford on the bus, Bloomsbury awoke on Professor Parchment's creaking sofa in Amnesia Cottage. He stumbled out into garden. His nose twitched eagerly at the scented freshness of the cool night air. He found a comfortable spot close to the water's edge and promptly went back to sleep. There he lay snoozing on the soft grass, rolling and twisting in tandem with his dreams.

Bloomsbury was riding a roller-coaster through the chaotic events that had unfolded since meeting up with Bodley in the Round Reading Room. The ground beneath him seethed with rats. Lights flashed and music blared. He could make head or tail of nothing, least of all his own conduct. He had behaved in a manner so unlike himself. On a daft and crazy impulse he had ditched the regular habits of a lifetime. All for the sake of a wild goose chase, which had pitched him from one harum-scarum happening to the next.

He was further tormented in this helter-skelter nightmare by fleeting appearances of Amenophis III, the Sakhmet Sisters and the Winged Lions of Nimrud. They all ignored his desperate attempts to enlist their help. Lady Caryatid drifted just beyond reach, with a haunting smile on her lovely lips. When Bloomsbury did succeed in coming close to her, she smartly turned her back on him. Meanwhile, pages of Parchment's stolen manuscript swirled about like so many leaves in a gale. He struggled to gather them together in the hope of saving the world, but he couldn't catch even one.

Bloomsbury's flagging spirits were sustained in his tormented dreams by the odd sighting of a certain diminutive rodent with a roguish manner and a waggish tongue in his head. In spite of himself, Bloomsbury pined for the company of this particular specimen of *rattus norwegicus*. Russell's courage, loyalty and true comradeship had touched him to the core. In his hour of need it was to this rare rat that he turned. But where was the little fellow? He was almost as elusive as the Great Bear himself. Then there followed terrible worries about Bodley: his young friend lost in a dark tunnel, far beyond any hope of rescue, and with the entire rat population of London after his blood.

Belinda found Bloomsbury tossing and turning on the lawn when she came out from the bee colony for her early shift on sentry duty. She was alarmed to find a big, brown bear where a couple of days previously there had been a smaller, golden version. The garden of Amnesia Cottage was becoming a right old bear garden and no mistake. The word must be getting around. After making a couple of low passes over his head, she buzzed in his ear.

"Wake up, wake up, whoever you are!"

"Bloomsbury opened an eye.

"What the ....? Who the ... ? Hold it. I say, you must be Belinda?"

The bumblebee was taken aback.

"I suppose Bodley has been passing on my personal details to the bear community at large. I mean, really, who can you trust nowadays?"

"Bodley would be here himself if he hadn't stayed on in London taking an enormous risk to help a mutual friend."

"You mean he didn't come back with Professor Parchment?"

"No, that's exactly what I'm saying."

"But I told him to stick to the Prof and all would be well. Why didn't he listen?"

"Bodley has turned out to be rather headstrong, I'm afraid."

"So where is Victor Verum?"

At the mention of the bookworm, Bloomsbury suddenly went quiet.

"I don't rightly know. He's gone missing. That's all I know. I can hardly think straight right now. Our dear friends are in the greatest danger. I've hardly slept a wink for worrying about them."

Bloomsbury gave Belinda a breathless account of their hair-raising adventures in London ending with the pursuit by the rats, the uncertain fate of heroic Russell and Bodley's equally heroic but unwise attempt to go after him. On top of all that there was Professor Parchment's stolen manuscript.

On hearing this, Belinda exclaimed.

"So that's why the Prof looks so miserable and sad. I've never seen him like that before. It's enough to break the hardest heart."

Belinda was about to pursue her enquiry about Victor Verum. But at that moment a pair of swans came sailing up the creek.

"I say, Belinda. These must be Bodley's friends Cedric and Celia. What a magnificent sight! Look, they are coming our way."

Bloomsbury introduced himself to the swans. The bear retold his unhappy tale at greater length, ending with a resounding list of Russell's brave deeds and noble qualities. The rat had rescued them not only from a horde of murderous rodents but also from the brutish Rottweiler. His last selfless act had been to do battle with the sharp-clawed British Museum cat. The swans curved their necks as they listened. Cedric offered a comforting thought.

"Sounds like a formidable character this Russell fellow. As for Bodley, he should be able to look after himself in a tight corner. So don't despair."

Bloomsbury nodded gravely.

"Yes, I do hope so. Bodley too has shown tremendous courage, and he's had plenty of bright ideas. Considering his youth, he has given a pretty good account of himself. So let's hope for the best."

A big shadow now spread across the lawn. They fell silent at the approach of Professor Parchment. He presented a distressing sight. His formerly cheerful, ruddy face was grey as ash, deeply etched with lines of sadness. He dragged his body along with the greatest effort. He made a slow tour of the garden and slumped off back into the house, a bent, broken man.

Long moments passed before Celia spoke.

"Oh dear! How awful! How terrible! All that on account of a stolen manuscript! It must be terribly important. We simply must help the Prof. I can't think of anything for the moment. But a change of air might give us some ideas. Why don't we all go out on the river? What do you think, Cedric?"

"An excellent notion, Celia my dear. Absolutely no point in moping about doing nothing. That never solved anything."

Bloomsbury settled himself on Cedric's back. He patted his white feathers as if plumping the cushions of his best armchair. So they set off and headed down the creek. But they hadn't gone far, when they heard an extremely excited high-pitched squeal coming from Parchment's garden.

"Wait for us! We've had a devil of a job getting here and we're not going to be left out of all the fun and games!"

All eyes turned towards the voice. Cedric and Celia paddled swiftly back to where Russell hopped about waving his arms. At his side Bodley was jumping up and down like a madman. He couldn't contain himself for sheer delight. Bloomsbury acted with a tad more decorum, but his heart also sang with joy at what he later described in his memoirs as this most felicitous reunion with his two best friends: the highly resourceful Russell Rat and the exceedingly brave Bodley.

"Stand back, I'm coming aboard!"

Russell sprinted across the lawn, sprang out over the water and made a light landing on Celia's back.

"So am I!"

Bodley followed. The two friends reached across to embrace Bloomsbury on Cedric's back. There was a great hugging of bears and rat. They quite forgot themselves and almost fell in the river.

"Russell, my dear friend, I had given you up for lost, eaten by the British Museum cat. What about you, Bodley? How did you get away? What happened after you left me? You must tell me the whole story."

Russell answered Bloomsbury with a potted version of his great escape. How he was about to be caught in Queen Square by the BM cat and then how he sorted the problem by enlisting the unwitting help of Reginald Rottweiler.

"Then I stumbled into this gaping hole in Queen Square. In a flash I knew for sure exactly how you two had landed on my doorstep. After that, I quickly guessed what had happened to Professor Parchment's manuscript."

All ears strained to hear the details.

"You remember, back there in the tunnel, before we set off for the Rat Race? How I told you to bring your luggage, and Bodley said you didn't have any?"

Bloomsbury nodded.

"Well, I didn't think anything of it at the time. Pretty dark down there, even for my sharp eyes. But it's clear I'd seen something. Anyway, to cut a long story short, I now realised that what I had thought was your luggage must have been the missing package with the Parchment Papers. I figured out it had fallen down the ventilation shaft just ahead of you two."

"So what did you do next?"

Russell tapped his head and then his palmtop PC to indicate it had been a mixture of raw ratty intelligence and cunning computer technology.

"First, I checked the co-ordinates. The spot up top by the hole in Queen Square corresponded exactly to where I had found you two down below on the Piccadilly Line. Hole in one, my old pals!"

"And then?"

Russell placed his nifty dark sunshades on his pointy nose. He was enjoying the suspense. So he kept Bloomsbury waiting.

"But what happened next, Russell? You did find the manuscript, didn't you?"

"Manuscript? Oh, yes. You could say I found it."

"So where is it?"

"All in good time, Bloomers old pal."

FRIENDS REUNITED

They were about to disappear around the first bend of the river when a loud cry came booming across the water. They turned to see the joyful spectacle of Professor Parchment dancing a jig on the lawn like a man possessed. He was brandishing aloft a brown paper package as if it were a prize trophy.

"Here it is, miraculously returned. My beloved manuscript. All is saved. It's not the end of the world. Merciful heavens! Bounteous providence!"

It did them all a power of good to see Professor Parchment instantly restored to his former cheery self. Bloomsbury's eyes turned enquiringly to Russell who communicated nothing beyond an innocent smile. Bodley maintained a discreet, knowing silence. Belinda could not hold back for a moment longer the question burning on the tip of her tongue.

"Where is Victor? You did find him, didn't you, Russell? He is all right, isn't he? Please tell!"

Russell inserted a paw into a waistcoat pocket and withdrew it a second later with the bookworm perched upon it. Victor Verum blinked in the bright sunshine. Belinda flew three circles around him to show how pleased she was to see him. Victor acknowledged her gesture with a gracious bow.

"Phew! Thought you'd never ask after *servitum vostrum*. Can't tell you what an ordeal I've been through. But in fact, I can tell you, thanks to our nice Mr Russell who came to my rescue. In the London Underground of all places! Can you imagine a worse place for an Oxford bookworm?"

As ever, Victor Verum was the first to answer his own questions.

"Well, of course you can't. So thank heavens, the excellent Mr Russell risked life and limb to find me. I'd almost reached the end of my tether when he freed me from the package. Don't know how long I'd been down there. But at least I had something to eat. The good old Parchment Papers kept me going."

At this, Bloomsbury grew alarmed.

"You didn't eat Professor Parchment's precious manuscript, did you?"

"Well, not exactly eat it. But I had to keep up my strength, didn't I? So I just took a little nibble here and there. I did munch carefully round the edges to leave the writing stuff. In case it was ever needed. I'd seen Parchment working on it, and I knew you were frightfully concerned about it. So I figured it must be important. Though I can't imagine why, can you?"

They looked at one another with huge relief.

"Anyway, as I was saying. I was at my wits end until Mr Russell turned up and set me free. Then he climbed up a deep shaft with *servitum vostrum* snug as a bug in his waistcoat pocket. It took simply ages to reach the top. He was carrying the Parchment Papers on his back, you see."

At this point Russell took up the tale.

"I nearly didn't make it. That run-around with the BM cat used up all my strength. I still had a long way to go up the ladder when I felt things slipping away. The manuscript weighed a ton. I would have had to let it drop or I'd have fallen back into the tunnel, and right into the arms of a hostile reception committee. It was that close. Touch and go. But for a certain person who appeared out of nowhere to give me a hand."

"A certain person?"

Bloomsbury, although he never did so himself, always liked others to get straight to the point.

"Well, do tell us, Russell. Get on with the story. Who was it?"

By way of an answer, Russell put an arm round Bodley's shoulders.

"This was the certain person who reached down and grabbed me in the nick of time. Then he hauled me up the ladder. Without him I would have been lost, and so would young Vic and the Parchment Papers. So really Bodley is the one to thank for everything at the end of the day. But he hasn't yet told me how he got there in the first place, and it's high time he did."

One moment basking in glory, the next Bodley was lost for words.

"Come on. Don't be shy."

"It was nothing really, Bloomsbury. When I left you in the Round Reading Room and went after Russell and the BM cat I hadn't a clue what I was doing. I just wanted to keep up with them, but they were much too fast for me. So I hid in a cardboard box. Russell kept racing round the block again and again, this way and that. Then I saw him whiz past on the final lap with the BM cat right behind before they rushed off to Queen Square. I arrived just in time to see Russell fall down the hole. Thought I'd better go down and see if he needed help. That's all. Nothing much to it really."

"That's all? Nothing much to it? What do you mean? That's amazing. Quite amazing. An outstanding effort. Well done, Bodley."

Bloomsbury's words of praise were music to his ears. Victor Verum now resumed the story.

"After that we took a ride on a suitcase with a nice Japanese tourist to the British Museum. Then Amenophis III sent the Sakhmet Sisters and the Pharaonic Cats to escort us to the bus stop in Trafalgar Square. Then the rats discovered us. They made Russell sing. They were planning to do him in afterwards. But the Sakhmet Sisters drove them crazy with an amazing concert. Boy, were they hot! The next big thing! Watch this space! Anyway, thanks to them we were able to slip away and catch the Oxford bus. Bodley knew the way to Parchment's place, so the rest was a doddle."

The mention of the Sakhmet Sisters reminded Russell of the bet. He pulled his palmtop PC from an inside pocket and offered it to Bloomsbury.

"Take it, Bloomers. You won the bet. Fair and square. The Sakhmet Sisters are really big, absolutely colossal. I mean seriously cool. Just as you predicted. That gig in Trafalgar Square was simply the best."

Still Bloomsbury hesitated.

"No thanks, Russell. I can't possibly take it."

Russell continued to hold it out.

"But I insist."

Bloomsbury could not bear to part Russell from his beloved palmtop PC.

"No, I wouldn't dream of it. Bears aren't meant to make bets, you know."

"Maybe not, Bloomers. But a bet is a bet. Even with a rat."

Bodley feared another session of the rat vs bear debate was about to start. So he was quite surprised by what happened next.

"Well, all right, Russell. So perhaps I should take it after all. So come on then, just hand it over, and let's settle the matter, there's a good chap."

Bloomsbury reached out to receive the palmtop PC from Russell's paw. Then he held it in his own for a few moments before speaking.

"But I do think you deserve a proper reward for your valuable part in saving the Parchment Papers, my dear Russell. Not to mention everything else you have done. So I have the greatest pleasure in making you a present of this handsome, this ingenious, this amazing piece of apparatus."

A great cheer went up. Russell smiled broadly from whisker to whisker as he accepted his precious palmtop PC and slipped it back into his pocket.

"So here's to peace and goodwill between rat and bear, Bloomers old pal."

"I'll shake on that, my dear Russell."

"All friends under the fur."

Cedric and Celia were feeling left out.

"All friends under fur and feathers!"

Then everyone joined in the chorus.

"All friends under fur and feathers!"

Bloomsbury looked about him in wonderment, as if he couldn't quite believe any of this was really happening. All these talking animals, and what they said actually made a great deal of sense.

"What adventures there are to be had in the big, wide world! Good gracious, is this the river we are floating on? Two bears and a rat on a swan's back. Not to mention a bee and a bookworm. What next?"

Cedric and Celia took Bloomsbury's remark as a real question.

"What next? I thought we had decided to have a day out on the river."

Bloomsbury beamed with pleasure.

"We had indeed so decided, and I must say it's still a most excellent idea."

Bodley thought so too.

"Yes, do let's have a day out on the river. Unless Bloomsbury would rather stay here and read the Professor's books or something?"

"Books, Bodley? Books? What are you thinking? Books indeed! There is a time for books, and there is a time for swanning about on the river. It is the mark of advanced wisdom to know which is which."

The old sparkle returned to Bloomsbury's eye.

"Today is so obviously made for swanning about on the river. Just the job for a real spot of cool, concentrated cogitation. Do you realise this stretch of water flows all the way to London? Now that is a thought to be thinking about. So let us be off. That is if you are quite ready, Cedric?"

"Absolutely. We'll take a long trip downstream. Though not as far as London, if you don't mind."

On this happy note, Cedric and Celia paddled off bearing their motley crew of merry passengers. The tiny flotilla was agog with joy and in a rare mood for celebration. It promised to be a grand day out on the river and one to remember for a long time to come.

Not surprisingly, they all felt that somehow they had reached the end of the story. In a sense they had. Dangers had been overcome. Good friends were reunited. The Parchment Papers had been found and restored to their owner. Furthermore, it seemed that the world had been saved, even though no one was quite sure how this had been achieved. But things didn't stop here. It was really just the end of another chapter, with various loose ends and some extremely important unfinished business yet to be sorted.

ON A SWAN'S BACK

Everyone had something to celebrate. But Bodley's joy had no limits.

"I can't begin to tell you all how glad I am to be back and to see everyone together. I was only away in London for a couple of days. But I began to believe I must have dreamed up all this: Amnesia Cottage, the garden, the river, everything. It was so strange."

Bloomsbury listened attentively.

"That is indeed most curious, Bodley. I do believe I am experiencing exactly the same thing. I only arrived in Oxford yesterday and already I find it almost impossible to imagine Amenophis III, the Sakhmet Sisters, the Winged Lions of Nimrud and Lady Caryatid or even the Round Reading Room of the British Museum at this precise moment. It makes me wonder whether anyone or anything can actually exist in a proper sense when you are far away and not able to confirm matters with your own eyes."

The light-hearted conversation had taken a more serious turn. Several minutes passed in silent reflection as they sailed downstream. Meanwhile, Bloomsbury's brain was ticking feverishly. He sensed a momentous idea coming into focus.

"All of which leads me nicely to the question young Bodley put to me when we met in the Round Reading Room. Who am I? He wanted to know who he was. Now I can tell him, if he still wants to know."

Bodley took a very deep breath. He had been expecting to hear the truth spoken from the fair lips of Lady Caryatid. But she was far away in London.

Bloomsbury was about to reveal all when he spotted a pair of Friesian cows munching the greenest grass right by the riverbank. Suddenly, he could not resist the temptation to spin things out with a gentle spot of pontificating on one of his pet subjects.

"Now, take those two black-and-white cows over there. We can see them now clear as day. So they must exist. No question about it. But soon we will be round the bend of the river and can no longer see them. What then? Will they still exist when we can't see them?"

Bodley recognised Daisy and Gertie. He gestured urgently to Bloomsbury to lower his voice for fear of offending the two formidable ladies. It was too late.

"As if we're about to vanish, Daisy!"

"Just because they're not here to make sure we really exist, Gertie!"

"Flaming cheek of it, Daisy!"

"A well aimed cowpat is what they need, Gertie."

"Shame they're out of range, Daisy."

Bloomsbury was too busy with the furious flow of his thoughts to register these remarks. Soon they rounded the bend in the river. Just as predicted, the cows were no longer visible. They had completely vanished! So did they or did they not exist?

Bloomsbury now became highly agitated. Then, in a blinding flash of genius, he felt he had cracked the riddle. He was elated, uplifted, inspired. So, standing on

Cedric's back and resting a paw on the swan's head to steady himself, he took a very deep breath.

"My very good friends of meadow and river. To celebrate the success of our adventures, I think we have earned a treat, a very special treat."

The animals raised a loud cheer in their eager anticipation that Bloomsbury would now shut up and they could all get on with enjoying themselves.

"So I propose to entertain and enlighten you all with a thumping good lecture!"

This was greeted with a loud groan. Bloomsbury didn't notice the change of mood.

"Perhaps it is the Oxford air. Or simply that the Big Idea is finally ripe and ready to fall on my head like a big juicy apple. Now listen carefully, my friends. For what I am about to reveal is the very pip of the aforesaid apple, the currant in the cake, the chocolate chip in the cookie, indeed nothing less than the writing in the rock and much else besides."

"Do get it over with, Bloomsbury!"

Bodley wasn't the only one thinking what Belinda whispered into his left ear. She smiled wearily across to Victor Verum, draped elegantly across the young bear's right ear. Even the talkative bookworm had been rendered speechless.

Undeterred, Bloomsbury launched headlong into his all-time greatest pontification. His words flowed sweet as honey, gleamed like pearls of wisdom, shone like golden coins of knowledge, sparkled like bright diamonds of understanding. The old bear glowed with excitement as he unlocked one door after another in his beautiful castle of truth. Bloomsbury approached his awesome conclusion just as the thatched roof of a riverside pub came into view and the creaking of an ancient signboard on rusty hinges added its own mysterious note to the proceedings.

"Now we have it within our grasp. Just one more step and we shall reach the peak of the magic mountain, the abode of the Great Bear himself. The final piece of the puzzle fell into place just now when I reflected on the existence or non-existence of those cows."

A great hush fell. Bloomsbury was on the point of revealing all. But at this critical moment the silence was shattered by an unexpected outburst of mooing. Although Daisy and Gertie were well out of sight, the booming voices of the cows bellowed loud and clear from a long way off over the becalmed river.

The effect on Bloomsbury was remarkable. His brain froze. His mouth stopped. The mental machine jammed. He just stood there on Cedric's back, utterly lost for words. Only his troubled eyes betrayed the frantic search going on inside his head for whatever it was he had been about to say.

Long moments passed in painful silence but for the occasional moo in the distance from Daisy and Gertie. At last Bloomsbury's lips started moving but the words they produced didn't amount to much. It was terrible to watch and listen. Although the argument had been understood by no one, yet all were shocked at his sudden loss of its thread. There followed an awkward silence, acutely embarrassing for everyone until at last, the bear regained his composure.

"I thought I had it all figured out. The Big Idea was right there in front of me. But a couple of moos and away it flew. Might never come back. I'm ever so sorry but the knowledge of the Great Bear is still beyond my reach. It always will be, I fear."

Stunned silence greeted this damp squib at the end of the lecture. It would have been a total disaster but for Russell's presence of mind. Standing on hind legs and with a paw resting on Bodley's shoulder for support while Celia sought to keep steady in the water, the rat proposed a vote of thanks. A great cheer arose. Bloomsbury basked in their rapturous applause. But this only encouraged him to deliver an encore.

"So permit me to conclude by saying what a marvellous bunch of chums you are. We are all in this together. The sun toasts our backs as we float in happy comradeship down the great river of life. That must surely be as wonderful as the Big Idea that just went down the swanny. I dare say there's a spot of lunch in prospect too. Who could possibly ask for more?"

Bloomsbury's audience rallied to him with the greatest enthusiasm at this point.

"So let us rejoice and make merry as we pour custard on the crumble and suck jam from the doughnut. May there always be toffee in the tin, corn on the cob, toad in the hole, floss on the candy, grass in the meadow, weeds in the pond, flowers in the garden, pollen in the petals, honey on the comb. Furthermore, for those with special dietary requirements ..."

Bloomsbury cast glance at Victor Verum.

"... stacks of books on the shelves."

The bookworm met his sparkling eyes with a grateful smile and a courteous *servitum vostrum*.

"So let us gild the lily, make hay while the sun shines and gather rosebuds while we may."

A tumultuous clapping of paws and beating of wings greeted this rousing finale. The entire company of animals congratulated the beaming Bloomsbury on what had been a luscious lecture, a dazzling disputation, a masterly monologue, a fabulous feast of philosophy, a silver-tongued soliloquy, a riot of riveting rhetoric. In short, a perfect peach of a speech.

Bodley was the only one to note how in his lecture Bloomsbury avoided answering the *who am I?* question. So perhaps Lady Caryatid would be the one after all to break the news? He breathed a sigh of relief. It would be so much better coming from her.

QUESTIONS AND ANSWERS

After Bloomsbury's amazing lecture things lightened up considerably. That summer turned out to be the finest in living memory. There was a magic spell in the air, which gave an extra sparkle to the sweetest of weather. One gorgeous day merged happily into the next as smoothly as two ripples on the river. With his lost manuscript restored, Professor Percival Parchment experienced a great surge of happiness. His work was saved. It would be published one day. But he didn't rush to send it off. Instead, he found untold joy idly browsing through his ragged bundle of papers.

So what had all the fuss and bother been about? They burned to know exactly what was in the manuscript that could possibly be so vital to the world. One morning, they all gathered together on the lawn of Amnesia Cottage by the side of the creek to rack their brains. Bodley was the first to hazard a guess.

"I reckon there must be secret clues hidden in the text leading to a vast treasure buried in a lost city somewhere in the middle of nowhere."

Bloomsbury didn't think much of that.

"You can't have somewhere in the middle of nowhere, Bodley. It doesn't make sense. Not logical. In the middle of somewhere, perhaps."

Belinda was convinced she knew better.

"It's much more likely to be a social study of bumble bees. The Prof used to watch us for hours."

At this, Cedric intervened.

"I dare say it could be a book about swans?"

Celia also favoured this possibility.

"Yes, the Professor always took such care to protect our nest and count the cygnets."

Russell threw his tuppence worth into the pot.

"Why not something about rats? With complete information on absolutely everything you've ever wanted to know about *rattus norwegicus.*"

Victor Verum had a completely different idea.

"All manuscripts taste pretty much the same when you eat them. So perhaps it doesn't really matter what's in the writing?"

Two black-and-white cows ambling past on the other bank of the river overheard the discussion.

"Who cares what it's all about, Daisy?"

"Just so long as we're not in it, Gertie."

"Who wants to be written about in some dusty old manuscript, Daisy?"

"Not me, Gertie."

"Nor me neither, Daisy."

The two cows continued their walk with flappers tightly shut in order to shield themselves from hearing any more stuff and nonsense.

Bloomsbury hadn't yet ventured a suggestion. Now they all turned to him, as if the learned bear alone could solve the big mystery of the Parchment Papers. Bloomsbury smiled knowingly. But when they pressed him, he came over all evasive.

"Well, let me begin and end by saying I really don't know. I haven't a clue."

This was most frustrating.

Then, with a sparkle in his eye, he added.

"But I do think it's high time we found out."

In order to resolve matters, Bloomsbury took it upon himself to *borrow* the manuscript. He read out loud to them all every single page of the Parchment Papers from start to finish. He accomplished this in instalments over several days while the professor was taking his afternoon nap. What they heard came as a big surprise for everyone.

The manuscript's full title was *SAND IN MY BOOTS*. It told the story of the professor's travels as a budding archaeologist many years ago. It was written like a diary of his daily adventures laced with jolly anecdotes about happy times with the desert people as they trekked through the sand from oasis to oasis, telling outrageous stories and cracking hilarious jokes along the way.

In fact, the jokes weren't all that funny, but the natural sense of humour behind them was rib-splittingly good. They laughed and chuckled from start to finish. It was such fun to listen to they hung on every word. When, in the end, it turned out young Parchment had made no great discoveries of lost cities or buried treasure, it didn't matter at all. Not one bit.

When he had finished, Bloomsbury looked over his half-moon spectacles.

"Well, my friends, we have all been barking up the wrong tree. It's not what any of us imagined. There is nothing here to save the world. But all the same Parchment has saved a lost world in his manuscript. I can see all the people he describes as if they were right before me: those wonderful characters riding endlessly into the sunset over the next sand dune. Parchment's crafty old cranium must have enough space for the entire Sahara and with plenty of room to spare. Who would have thought it possible?"

Bloomsbury patted the manuscript. At that very moment Professor Parchment stepped out of the house. He no longer looked to them like an old man who had never been young. They viewed him with fresh respect as they imagined all those camels plodding to and fro in a vast wind-swept desert of memory stretching between his ears. Russell wondered how many DVDs it would take to store everything that was filed away inside the Prof's ancient head under its flowing mane of snow-white hair.

After solving the mystery, or rather the non-mystery, of the Parchment Papers, Bloomsbury finally seemed to lose all interest in his own search for Truth with a capital T. Probably on account of his unfinished lecture on a swan's back, there was no more talk of the Big Idea. Much to Bodley's relief, he did not even mention taking a stroll down Pontification Parade or a hike up Homework Hill. Bodley hoped that his small act of deception in luring his friend to Oxford might yet go completely undiscovered.

However, the heady academic atmosphere of Oxford did affect Bloomsbury in a rather unexpected manner. He was absolutely thrilled to be staying here in this celebrated city of words. His whole being buzzed with such excitement that his great brain seemed to acquire a mind of its own. In short, Bloomsbury began to behave in a most unusual way.

He would be overcome by strange fits, lasting for hours on end. For example, he would use only words starting with a certain letter, depending which day of the week it was. One Monday, he greeted them all with a most amazing salutation.

"Magnificent midsummer morning my merry mates, methinks."

He continued to speak in the same vein until stopping for lunch. Bloomsbury's weird way with words was wonderfully winning. Which is precisely how he spoke one Wednesday.

Occasionally, Bloomsbury would serve up as a nice breakfast treat what he described as horrendously huge helpings of hyperbole laced with no small measure of litotes. He encouraged everyone to learn from him. Very soon his classes in advanced practical pontificating became a hit for miles around.

Gradually, individual words started to come unstuck in the heat of his fevered mind. Then they fell into tiny pieces. *Abundance*, for example, broke down into *a bun dance*. He wondered who on earth was responsible for putting the *pun* in the *Punjab*. And what about the *jab* for that matter? Bloomsbury would laugh so uproariously at these feeble jokes he didn't notice that the others failed to join in. His increasingly odd behaviour caused everyone much concern. Russell reckoned he had picked up a nasty virus that sort of scrambled his ursine brain cells. Then one fine day, Bloomsbury surprised them all by announcing that he had finally reached mental meltdown.

"Do you know what, my friends? I reckon all this cool, concentrated cogitation has just about worn out the cogs in my brain."

As if to prove it, the bear invited them all to gather round under the shade of an old oak tree near the river. He harrumphed to clear his throat.

"I'm going to tell you a story the like of which has never been heard. It's all about talking animals. So it should be right up your street."

All ears pricked up with curiosity as Bloomsbury harrumphed once more and began. A very strange tale it was too.

"That gets my goat, exclaimed the stoat. We're going to sneeze, announced the fleas. I'm wide-awake, hissed the snake. I'll come of course, agreed the horse. Who nicked my socks? Asked the fox. A cup of tea? Enquired the bee. Slept like a log, barked the dog. You do look pale, remarked the snail. I like your perm, whispered the worm. See you anon, added the swan. It's going to snow, croaked the crow. My boy goes to Harrow, bragged the sparrow. Upon my soul, avowed the vole. I'll eat my hat, declared the rat."

Bloomsbury recited all this in great earnest. But the animals were not hugely amused.

"But that's not a proper story."

Bloomsbury beamed with satisfaction, as if that reaction was precisely what he had been expecting and hoping for. With a broad grin, he retorted.

"Well, I don't care, said the bear."

There was a longish silence before Bloomsbury burst out laughing.

"I don't care, said the bear. Get it? I don't care, said the bear. That's the punch line!"

Bloomsbury was still the only one laughing.

"Shall I tell it again from the beginning?"

Bloomsbury laughed again. This time they all joined in but only out of politeness. Their painful looks confirmed the general feeling that he had finally gone off his rocker. Afterwards, Bodley took Bloomsbury aside and asked him if he was feeling alright.

"Many a true jest is spoken in earnest, Bodley. That little bit of doggerel was just to confuse serious people who read too much into the book."

"The book? What book?"

"Life, my dear Bodley, is like a book. Every day presents us with a new page. The things we do are the writing on the page. We don't have to keep a diary like Parchment. Our actions fill the pages all by themselves. So we are all authors writing our life story every single day of the year. But we can only guess at what lies beyond the covers of the book we are writing. We cannot even know whose bookshelf we are on."

"But will other people ever read our story? Will anyone be interested?"

"Maybe. Maybe not. That is not the point. We have to keep filling the pages regardless whether anyone else is interested or not. We must do it in the very best way we can. For the Great Bear himself always reads every line of our life story over our shoulder."

Suddenly, Bloomsbury remembered something.

"That brings me to what I wanted to tell you about the *who am I?* question. Who you are is simple. It's what you do and how you do it. Name and address, place and date of birth, forms and certificates, height and weight and suchlike and so on and so forth etc are all very well. But none of those details really matter. You may or may not be called Bodley. That just happens to be the name by which I know you. But I know who you are even without knowing your name. You have conducted yourself very well, been brave, stood by your friends. So no worries, as Russell would say. No worries at all. Just carry on writing the story of your life page by page. No one can ask more than that. The rest will take care of itself."

Bodley felt a huge weight lifted from his shoulders. He smiled. Bloomsbury instantly became merry and light-hearted again. After that he behaved pretty much the same as everyone else. More often than not, the old bear was the one leading the others astray with silly pranks and jolly japery. In fact, very little cogitation - cool, concentrated or otherwise - was done that summer. In its place came fun, frolics and the simple pleasures of easy-going comradeship. Just like the good folk in the Parchment Papers.

There was always something exciting going on. Cedric and Celia were kept busy ferrying everyone up and downstream on various outings. One weekend, they made the long journey all the way to the big house at the source of the river. But when they finally arrived, there was no one at home. All they found was a scribbled note informing all visitors that Old Father Thames had gone swimming to keep cool.

As for Russell, he still checked his emails from time to time but with less and less interest. Slowly his PC battery ran down. One day, when he switched it on, the screen remained blank. So he couldn't download the latest news from *www.russellratwanteddeadoralive.com.* The formerly hyperactive cyber rat hid his palmtop PC in an old tree stump and thought no more about it. After a while he even forgot where it was, and he didn't miss it at all. He had discovered it was a million times more fun swanning about on the river with his pals than cruising the wildest galaxies of cyberspace or tracking every single move of the Global Index.

In truth, Russell had never shared the same career ambitions as the rest of the rat pack. Deep down he lacked the hard-nosed drive essential to success in rodent society. So he fell quite easily into the laid-back rhythm of his new life and soon became a popular figure on the social circuit, not least for his story telling.

He quickly lost count of the number of times he was asked to narrate the exciting tale of his daring mission down into the deep, dark tunnel of the Piccadilly Line and how he had rescued Victor Verum and the Parchment Papers from the gnashing teeth of his angry fellow rodents. Bodley's heroic part always received a full and proper mention.

Every time Bodley heard the story, he dearly wished he was back there in person for the wonderful ride down Regent Street on the back of a fabulous Pharaonic Cat. Best of all, he loved the final scene in Trafalgar Square when the divine Sakhmet Sisters sang their hearts out and created the perfect diversion for a thrilling getaway. With each telling, Russell's story became more dramatic as he remembered and invented yet more and more gripping details.

Bodley thought often of the lovely Lady Caryatid and wondered what it was she would have told him in reply to the *who am I?* question. Would it have been the same as Bloomsbury's answer? But deep down he was no longer concerned to dwell on who he was. Or rather on who he might have been. He was simply so happy that it didn't matter. In fact, he had given up asking questions altogether. Things were fine just as they were. Couldn't be better.

He had discovered that a pair of swans could make perfect parents, a bumblebee and a bookworm the craziest of cousins. A rare rodent was the best possible best friend under the sun. Even a couple of quarrelsome cows could stand in pretty passably as grumpy great aunts. As for a certain older fellow bear, he provided all the ancestors he ever needed rolled into one. In short, the whole world was his family.

Bodley was high on happiness. He walked about in a blur of bliss most of the time, with Belinda buzzing in one ear and Victor Verum curled up snugly behind the other. They exchanged knowing smiles quite often, especially when Bodley uttered his favourite salutation, freely delivered to all and sundry.

"*Servitum vostrum.* Gosh, how wonderful to see you, and suchlike and so forth and so on, et cetera."

This became simply the coolest thing to say that year in Oxford, when greeting either friend or stranger.

DOUBLE CRIPES!!

As for absent-minded Professor Parchment, things don't get any better. Occasionally, the old man would even forget that his lost manuscript has been found and he starts to look for it all over again. Generally, the confusion doesn't last too long since he has stuck little notes everywhere to remind him the precious papers are locked away safe and sound in the bottom drawer of his desk. But the professor still can't recall the most important fact, namely that his great-nephew Tom is meant to be staying with him.

However, he does seem aware something is not quite as it should be. He often mops his brow with a big, red handkerchief and scratches his head as if trying to solve a really difficult puzzle. Sometimes Professor Parchment looks intensely at the spot where Bodley is standing, as if he can almost see him as a vague shape shimmering on the edge of his vision. But when the professor cleans his spectacles and looks again no one is there. Bodley for his part, when he studies Professor Parchment at close quarters, feels sure he knows him from somewhere else, perhaps another world or former life, but the exact memory always evades him.

Meanwhile, one fine summer day follows another as the long, hot days peel off the calendar one by one. Bodley is the last to notice summer green merge into autumn gold. A fresher wind now stirs the reeds along the riverbank. On one such breezy morning something happens that turns his cosy little world upside down and stands everything right on its head.

A picture postcard drops through the letterbox of Amnesia Cottage and lands softly on the doormat. The stamps announce it is from a country in Africa. Nothing remarkable in that. Professor Parchment is always receiving exotic communications from old friends in foreign parts. But this one is different. It contains a few words from Tom's parents to the effect that they have had a really grand time on their African expedition. They now look forward so very much to calling by to collect their darling son.

As the professor reads and re-reads the card, his ruddy face drains of colour. Tom? Tom! So that was the enormously important matter he had forgotten all about! His very own great-nephew!

"Cripes!"

How could he have been so stupid?

"Double cripes!!"

Then the awful truth sinks in.

"By the beard of Amenophis! I've really done it this time. Where is the dear boy?"

In mounting panic he runs from room to room.

"Tom! Tom! Where are you, Tom?"

The empty house echoes to the frantic cries of Professor Parchment. He rushes upstairs to the tiny attic box-room which he now clearly remembers was where he cleared a space among the piles of books for the young boy to sleep.

"Tom! Tom! Are you there?"

Answer comes there none. No one present. Just furtive, sideways looks from spiders squatting on their webs in dusty corners of the window panes. The only sign of Tom's brief residence here is a small, brown suitcase. The professor opens it with trembling hand, fearful what he might find. But the few personal possessions – Swiss army knife, piece of string, blunt pencil, exercise book for some neglected piece of holiday homework – provide no clue as to Tom's whereabouts. They merely confirm the awful truth that Professor Parchment has been so utterly lacking in his responsibilities to the boy that he has allowed him to disappear without even noticing.

How long has Tom been gone? When did he last see him? The old man racks his memory. The last thing he can recall with absolute certainty is a visit to a gift shop in the Bodleian Library. But when? It must have been many days, or was it weeks previously?

He trudges downstairs, cradling Tom's suitcase in his arms. He slumps in despair on the sofa. If only he hadn't been so wrapped up with his blessed manuscript. He knows that losing Tom is a hundred thousand times worse than losing the story of his life. He wants to grab the perishing papers and throw them out of the window. If it hadn't been for his obsession with them, his great-nephew would still be right there with him. But what should he do now? Call the police? What on earth would he tell them when they ask him: *"When precisely did you last see your great-nephew?"*

Only then, thinking of the police, does it occur to Professor Parchment that Tom might be in danger. He prays no harm has come to the boy. But he fears the worst. Suddenly, the old man can take it no more. He is overwhelmed by the awfulness of what he has done. He holds his head between his hands and begins to sob. Gently at first, but then with complete abandon, the tears flow like a mighty river. Thus it is that he fails to hear the ringing of his doorbell. At last, he recognises the voices of Tom's parents shouting.

"Hallo! Hallo! Anyone at home?"

The professor can hardly move. It is like the very worst nightmare. Every single movement requires a tremendous, superhuman effort, like walking with heavy boots through sticky treacle. Finally, he manages to get up and totter unsteadily towards the front door. What on earth will he tell Tom's parents?

The dramatic turn of events unfolding inside the house passes completely unnoticed by the congenial company gathered outside in the garden of Amnesia Cottage. Bodley, Russell, Victor Verum and Belinda are sitting in a half circle around Bloomsbury. While Cedric and Celia follow proceedings floating on the water of the creek close to the bank.

Clearly an important matter is just about to be announced, for Bloomsbury has been harrumphing all morning in that peculiar way of his which invariably indicates something of great significance is afoot. Bloomsbury now clears his throat and harrumphs again with particular emphasis.

"Well, Bodley. I must say, that was a happy holiday, a beautiful break, a valuable vacation and so on and so forth and suchlike etc. But now it is time for more serious matters. I am ready for that stroll down Logic Lane, then a saunter along Pontification Parade and all those other wonderful streets you promised. Afterwards, I shall finally quench my great thirst for knowledge at the hostelry of *The Great Bear*."

Bodley winces. Bloomsbury has remembered after all. His lies and deceptions will be exposed.

"Then it will be high time we headed back to London. There must be a mountain of work awaiting us in the Round Reading Room."

Bodley gulps.

"Awaiting *us*? Well, er ..."

"Yes, you are my new Research Assistant. Or have you already forgotten?"

Bloomsbury seeks to encourage him.

"Won't it be marvellous to see all our old friends in the British Museum?"

Bodley thinks of Lady Caryatid. He is seized by a massive, simply overwhelming desire to see her again. He has never forgotten her solemn promise to answer his question. Now he is ready to hear who he is. In spite of what Bloomsbury has said, he really wants to know all the details about himself. He simply aches to find out where he really belongs.

That is his last conscious thought before he feels something like a sharp jolt inside his head. The kind of thing that happens when your foot misses the very last step on the way downstairs in the dark. Now he has a vague memory of standing in a passage outside a door in the middle of the night. He can hear voices inside. But then, all of a sudden, his mind goes blank.

Meanwhile, Tom's parents have given up waiting for Professor Parchment to open the front door. They have taken the side way into the garden.

"Tom! Tom! It's us. We're back from Africa. We're here. We've come to collect you."

The garden appears to be empty.

"Tom! Tom! Where are you?"

At first, the young boy lying on the grass all on his own by a tree stump right next to the water's edge doesn't hear them. That's because he is partly still in a different world. But now the sound of familiar voices calling out what he recognises to be none other than his very own name penetrates his consciousness.

"Tom? That's my name, isn't it? Tom, that's who I am! I'm Tom! Yes, that's me! I'm here!"

"Tom! Tom! There you are! We're back! We've come to take you home."

The young boy scrambles to his feet. He sprints headlong into the outstretched arms of a smiling, laughing, hugging man and woman.

"Mum! Dad!"

"Tom! Tom! How wonderful to see you! We've missed you so much."

The happy family reunion soon gives way to the usual parental enquiries.

"Have you been behaving yourself? What have you been up to? How was the weather? Where is your great-uncle Percy, by the way?"

The three of them now turn to see the shuffling approach of the old man, sobbing and sniffling, his nose buried deep in a big, red handkerchief. Having found no one at the front door, he has come into the garden. He stops in his tracks. What's this? Tom? Tom! Not missing after all? What's going on? He can't believe the boy is really here. Between sobs he mumbles a few words of greeting.

"Everyone here? All present and correct?"

He looks at Tom in disbelief. Then at last he does believe that his great-nephew is really there.

"Oh, how wonderful! How truly wonderful! How amazingly wonderful to see you all together! Do excuse my wet eyes. I must look a proper state. All on account of this perishing hay fever, you know. Never had this problem out in the desert. No pollen, you see. I'll be all right in a moment."

He pats Tom lightly on the head several times, then squeezes his arm, just to make sure he is real. He struggles to contain his tears.

"You don't know what this means to me. Really you don't."

Tom's Mum responds with an understanding smile in order to give the impression she knows exactly what's going on. But she hasn't a clue. She has never seen great-uncle Percy as emotional as this. She reckons she'll get more sense from her son.

"Now, Tom do tell us what the two of you have been up to all summer."

"Well, er…"

The young boy appears strangely uncertain how to respond to his mother's simple question. So she now turns instead to great-uncle Percy.

"I trust our Tom has been no trouble?"

"Trouble? Tom? Tom? Trouble?"

She eyes him suspiciously. He seems a bit confused. Finally, the old man decides he can truthfully say that Tom hasn't caused any trouble. If only because he can't even remember him being there.

"No. Tom no trouble. No trouble at all."

Tom's Mum now looks at great-uncle Percy as if he were a half-wit. Or possibly drunk. But what else can the poor man say? Not much. He is mute, speechless, struck dumb. Young Tom, whom he had assumed lost and gone forever, and all thanks to his total neglect of the boy, now stands before him. It must be some kind of miracle. What on earth is going on?

Great-uncle Percy's mind buzzes with questions. Perhaps his absent-mindedness has played an elaborate game of double bluff, making him think he had lost his great-nephew while he had been there all the time? But try as he might to believe this, things simply don't make sense. Nothing adds up. He knows he can't leave it at that. Tom's parents expect a fuller account.

"We got along quite brilliantly the two of us. Simply splendidly, doing this and that, and we had a grand time together, didn't we young man?"

He looks anxiously at the boy, pleading with him to confirm this. Now Tom is on the spot.

"Well, er…"

Tom's parents slowly shake their heads. Their son seems more tongue-tied than ever. Communication skills just as bad as before. No improvement there. The stay with great-uncle Percy is promptly marked down as a failure on that score. Now they focus on the old man bravely trying to concoct a story.

"Yes, I'm sure we had a grand time. I showed him all over Oxford. Took him everywhere. Don't expect me to remember the names of all the places we went together. Though I do recall taking him to the Bodleian Library. I thought with a name like Thomas Bodley he would want to read lots of big old dusty books. Isn't that right, young man?"

Tom nods, but still he cannot speak. Bodley? Thomas Bodley? Bodley! The mention of his real name stirs up a whirlpool of emotion. His mind is in turmoil. He can't yet see anything clearly. Then suddenly, he recalls something of the utmost urgency.

Without a word, Tom turns on his heels, dashes across the lawn at top speed and races down to the water's edge. But he is no longer sure who or what he is looking for so desperately. Then, far away, he spots two white swans. Their graceful necks arch back towards him for a brief moment just as they vanish from sight. He goes to call after them, only to find their names do not spring to his lips as he expects them to. A distant memory sparkles. But obstinately, rather like a damp match, it refuses to ignite.

More perplexed than ever, Tom returns to his parents. On the way back he bends down to pick up a small teddy bear he sees lying on the grass by a tree stump. He picks it up and looks at it intently, as if it alone can tell him what he wants to know. But the bear remains silent. It is only a stuffed toy.

A teddy bear? Tom's parents shake their heads again. Their son hasn't grown up at all. Another bad mark goes down against him.

"Surely we agreed we're a bit old for teddy bears, Tom? Did we not?"

He feels extremely foolish. He would like the ground to swallow him up. But now great-uncle Percy unexpectedly comes steaming to the rescue.

"I don't think you can ever be too old for bears. Anyway, it's all my fault. Tom wasn't interested. But I insisted. Couldn't resist buying him this one. From the gift shop at the Bodleian Library of all places."

Tom's Mum is secretly asking herself whether great-uncle Percy has been such a good influence. But she decides to be diplomatic.

"Well, that does make it rather special, I suppose. But all the same…"

She turns again to her son with what she thinks is a safe question.

"Now Tom, tell me at least you have been eating properly, haven't you?"

Even this causes Tom a considerable problem. He can't remember eating anything at Amnesia Cottage since those dry biscuits and glass of cold milk the very first evening. So when he does manage to speak it's as if he isn't quite sure where the words are coming from.

"Oh yes, I ate very well. Some days we even had as a very special treat for breakfast huge helpings of hyperbole and no small measure of litotes and ... er ..."

Tom's Mum and Dad exchange worried glances. They don't have a clue what their son is talking about. Is he making fun of them?

They look to great-uncle Percy for some kind of an explanation. The old man shrugs his shoulders. He is thinking hard. Hyperbole and litotes for breakfast, indeed? Clearly, there is more to his great-nephew than he has supposed. Intrigued, great-uncle Percy bends down with a creaking of professorial knees and looks Tom firmly in the eye. He likes what he sees.

"Now tell us what all that is supposed to mean, young man?"

Tom stands there, totally bewildered by what he has said. Could hyperbole and litotes be new brands of breakfast cereal perhaps? Where on earth did he get the strange words? He looks deep into great-uncle Percy's eyes. They are wise and warm and kind. They remind him of someone. Then suddenly he has a thought. No, it's more like a flash of inspiration. Bloomsbury! Bloomsbury would know! Why hadn't he remembered him before? Yes, dear old, good old, clever old Bloomsbury! Of course!! Of course!!!

He shuts his eyes and concentrates hard. The mists of forgetfulness start to clear. Now he can see. In a wonderful great rush everything and everyone come back to him in a gushing flood of beautiful memories. Bloomsbury, Russell, Victor Verum, Belinda, Cedric and Celia. He recalls the fun, frolics and dangers of their escapades. Lionel and Leopold, Amenophis III, the Sakhmet Sisters, and the lovely Lady Caryatid. They all pass before him one by one.

Only after they have departed, does Tom realise they were taking their leave of him. He will see them no more. Tears roll down his cheeks like a river of sadness which carries all his companions away. Tom hides his face in his hands so his parents can't see he's crying. That's the last thing he wants.

Now the tears stop as suddenly as they started. Tom breathes a huge sigh of happiness, overjoyed that the memory of his dear friends has been restored to him. Just to make sure he will remember them all, he repeats their names over and over again, securing their faces in his mind. He promises never to forget a single one of them, not even for a second.

MEETING OF MINDS

At last, Tom takes a deep breath, opens his eyes and smiles triumphantly. Three pairs of adult eyes are trained expectantly on his, waiting for him to speak. He notes something decidedly swan-like in the enquiring way his parents have arched their necks towards him. Then there is something rather ursine, and distinctly Bloomsburyish, to the learned, thoughtful expression with which great-uncle Percy is studying him. Suddenly his words gush forth without much rhyme or reason.

"I say, Mum, Dad. How wonderful to see you. Really missed you. *Servitum vostrum* and suchlike and so forth and so on, et cetera. I've had a fantastic time. Absolutely marvellous. It's been just one adventure after another. Never a dull moment. Great-uncle Percy took me to London."

The old man's jaw drops.

"To London?"

"Yes, to see Leopold and Lionel and ... "

"Leopold and Lionel?"

"The Winged Lions of Nimrud, you know."

Tom's parents turn to great-uncle Percy.

"You took Tom to London?"

The old man turns to Tom. The boy nods.

"I did?"

Tom nods again and throws an enormous wink. Even so, it takes great-uncle Percy ages to get the hint.

"Did I? Didn't I? I mean, yes. Yes, I did! I did! Of course I did! Didn't I just?"

Tom then tells a carefully edited account of the lost manuscript. According to his version of events, great-uncle Percy mislaid it somewhere and completely forgot where he had left it. But Tom made a clever guess that it was somewhere in the Underground Station at Russell Square. So he went back to fetch it for him. That was all. Nothing to it really. Tom doesn't mention Bloomsbury, Russell or anything out of the ordinary. He reckons there are some things his parents won't even begin to understand.

Great-uncle Percy nods occasionally as he listens to Tom's story. It all rings true. Yes, he did lose his manuscript in London, didn't he? Then somehow it was returned to him, wasn't it? So it appears he has his great-nephew to thank for it. But how on earth did Tom manage that? The confused old man decides it's best to let the young boy do the talking.

"Exactly so, it was all just as Tom says. It's far better if you hear all the details from him. My memory being what it is, you know."

Tom has plenty of other things to say.

"Fancy great-uncle Percy being a close friend of everyone worth knowing in the British Museum. Lady Caryatid, Amenophis III and the Sakhmet Sisters! Really cool. Awesome. Unbelievable."

Unbelievable, that's the word the old man is looking for to describe Tom's breathless account. But he says nothing. Instead, he basks in the warm rays of his great-nephew's praise. He listens in utter rapture at all the things they have done together, from jolly outings on the river to moonlight visits of the British Museum. It isn't long before he comes to believe that he and Tom have actually enjoyed a simply rollicking time together right through the summer holiday. He starts jumping up and down on the lawn as excitedly as any young lad.

Tom's parents become most alarmed at the sudden boyish enthusiasm of great-uncle Percy. They also feel completely left out of things. Why has no one bothered to ask them about their daring expedition to Africa? Dad decides it's high time to remind them of where they've been and what they've done.

"I bet you're just dying to hear all about our African adventures? The Congo, the Limpopo. All the places I've ever dreamed of."

Before he can stop himself, Tom is singing and dancing like the Sakhmet Sisters.

"You can bongo on the Congo,
Sip cocoa on the Limpopo.
Or take it nice and easy
On the shores of the Zambezi.
But nothing beats the smile
Of a sunrise on the Nile."

Great-uncle Percy can't help himself joining in and shouting *hurrah! hurrah!* and causing Tom's parents great concern for his sanity. Mum takes Dad aside.

"I don't think Tom has grown up at all."

"No, and if anything he has managed to get his great-uncle Percy behaving like a schoolboy."

Tom's Mum comes closer to the truth than she realises when she says.

"I would have thought they might have tired of one another's company by now. But it feels like they've only just met."

Tom's Dad agrees.

"Yes, that's rather odd, isn't it?"

Tom's parents have arranged to stay on a couple of days longer at Amnesia Cottage before they take their son home. During this time, they find themselves left mostly on the sidelines while the old man and the young boy hit it off like the best of pals. In fact, they are thick as thieves. Great-uncle Percy gets so carried away with Tom's tales of life on the riverbank, he even starts remembering things that hadn't happened. Like the time they sat up all night by a campfire with Old Father Thames telling his tall stories. Tom politely lets these little inventions pass without comment.

As for Tom, he is happier than he can ever remember. He can't quite get over knowing that his real name is Thomas Bodley. So in this sense he reckons he has really been who he really is all along. Even though he hadn't known who he was, he had still been who he was meant to be. Or something like that? It sounds like the sort of puzzle only Bloomsbury could solve.

The one big cloud on the horizon is going home. He consoles himself with the fact he will bring back with him a companion for Arthur. But Amnesia

Cottage, Oblivion Avenue, Oxford now feels like his real address. It is the magic place that connects him to everyone and to everything.

On the other hand, certain things aren't the same any more. Cedric and Celia won't respond to his greetings. They will insist on remaining silent and behaving in a distant manner, as if they are just normal, ordinary swans. Nor is Belinda to be seen buzzing around the flowers. Tom tells himself she might be working nights. But he suspects she is lying low what with so many adult humans about. As for Bloomsbury, Russell and Victor Verum, there is not the slightest trace. Perhaps they have already set off for London? Tom is most perplexed. It feels to him almost as if they have never existed.

He finds unexpected comfort in the company of great-uncle Percy. They speak often of their mutual acquaintances in the British Museum.

"By the beard of Amenophis, Tom. I can't tell you how good it is to converse with someone of your age. So refreshing. Why, you talk about Amenophis III, the Winged Lions of Nimrud, Lady Caryatid and the Sakhmet Sisters as if you knew them all personally. As if they were still alive and well."

"But surely they are alive and well, aren't they?"

The old man reflects deeply.

"Well, if you feel they are still alive and well, then yes. I suppose they must be."

Tom isn't entirely happy with this answer. There must be more to it than that. It was all so real. He

224

desperately wants to tell all about his adventures with Bloomsbury, Russell, Victor Verum, their narrow escape from the rats and the real saga of the lost manuscript. Most important of all, he is burning to tell the truth about his disappearance and transformation. He needs to confide in someone. Finally, he decides he really must speak to great-uncle Percy.

"I've been meaning to tell you something ..."

But first the old man has something on his mind that he wants to confide to Tom.

"And I've been meaning to tell you something, Tom. I don't know whether you've noticed, but more often than not I can't tell what day of the week it is. My days of cool, concentrated cogitation are well and truly behind me. So you must forgive me if I appear a bit absent-minded at times. Why, to be honest, I can't remember even half the things we got up to over the summer. At least not half as clearly as you. So it's good to have you on hand to remind me. Curious thing, the human mind. Can play awful tricks, you know. Do you realise what happened once? I think I thought you had disappeared. Or that I had mislaid you, or somehow forgotten about you. Can you imagine?"

"Oh, really?"

"Oh, yes. If I had really done that, I don't think I could ever forgive myself. But it turned out I was mistaken. Just a trick of the mind. You were there all the time. Thank heavens for that."

Tom smiles, but he says nothing.

"What was it you wanted to tell me, Tom?"

225

Tom decides not to tell his true story after all. Best leave things as they are. Perhaps a small dose of forgetfulness can sometimes be a good thing.

"Well, I'm not really sure. That is, I don't know. It's gone. I think I must have forgotten."

"Now don't you start forgetting things too. One scatterbrain in the family is quite enough."

They laugh like schoolboys. Then the professor turns a shade more serious.

"Hold on, Tom. I've remembered something else. You know when you first arrived at Amnesia Cottage? Well, the moment I saw you I saw myself as I once was, a young boy just like you starting out in life, head full of wonderful dreams. Realised immediately how dull I had allowed myself to become. I knew there wasn't an ounce of fun in my manuscript. But your arrival inspired me. All the happy memories came flooding back. So I rewrote the whole thing. From start to finish. Kept me busy I can tell you, confoundedly busy. Had to work like mad to get it all written down before I forgot about it all over again."

So that was why great-uncle Percy had been so totally wrapped up with his manuscript. Tom would never have guessed.

"So I have you to thank for that. I would have told you this earlier. But I've only just remembered. Then there's something else I have to tell you. I'm not going to start another book. This one was special. It's made me realise there's more to life than scribbling.

226

What's left is for action. It's what you do in life that counts even more than what you write."

Now where had Tom heard something like that recently?

"So I shall dedicate *SAND IN MY BOOTS* to you. Without you it wouldn't be the same. I'd better do it straight away before I forget."

"Wow! To me? Gosh, really? Cool. Thanks."

"I've learned a lot from you, Tom. Curious that you have to become seriously old before you can understand what it means to be foolishly young, isn't it? The folks in between really don't get it, do they?"

"Folks in between?"

"You know, the adults."

"Oh them. Who wants to be an adult?"

"You'll have to become one too, I'm afraid. But just look on the bright side. The sooner you grow up, the sooner you can grow down."

"Grow down? That sounds like fun."

"It is. Believe me. It is."

So great-uncle Percy has finally managed to get things off his chest. He breathes deep to savour the the happy moment. Just then an enormous sneeze wells up inside him and the big, red handkerchief comes out of his pocket in double-quick time.

"Aaaaaaatishooooooo!!!"

Two smaller sneezes follow in rapid succession.

"Perishing pollen. Never suffered from hay fever in the desert."

Suddenly great-uncle Percy's eyes light up.

227

"The desert? The desert! Why didn't I think of that before? I reckon there's another safari in me. At least one. Possibly more."

Then the old man's eyes light up even brighter.

"Fancy a spot of desert exploration, Tom? We could go together. What a lark that would be."

Tom can't speak for excitement.

"Yes, let's go travelling, Tom. Perhaps we could search for the missing beard of Amenophis III? It's something I've wanted to do for ages and I have a very shrewd idea where to look. I didn't mention it in the book in case some one else gets there first."

"The beard of Amenophis III! He'll be ever so pleased to get it back."

"So what do you say? Would you like to come?"

"What do I say? I say gosh, terrific, cool, brilliant, ace. Cripes! Double cripes!! Triple cripes!!! Just wait till I tell Mum and Dad."

Tom stops right there when he realises the flaw in the plan.

"But they're bound to say I'm too young or make some silly excuse or other."

"Just leave it to me, Tom. Best not say anything for the moment. I'll make some arrangements, contact a few people. I'll put it to your parents at just the right moment and then we'll go for it."

"Promise?"

"Promise."

Tom gives his great-uncle a great hug.

Now a movement on the creek catches his eye.

"Gosh, look over there! It's the swans! Let's go and see them!"

Happily at peace with himself and the whole wide world, the old man follows the young boy down to the water's edge. Tom's parents watch them from the house. They wonder why their son is so interested in swans. They are sure they've even seen him trying to talk to this particular pair always hanging about in the creek. Reading books about talking animals is bad enough. But actually talking to animals in real life must be a worrying sign of something. They do hope this curious phase will pass when they get Tom home. And the sooner the better in their view.

So had all his adventures really happened? Once home, Tom can't be totally sure of this or indeed of anything. Sometimes, as if hoping for an answer, he stares and stares at this mysterious bear from the Bodleian Library, for Bodley is now cosily ensconced on a shelf above Tom's bed alongside Arthur, whom he has fetched down from his exile in the attic.

When they catch him like this, still communing with teddy bears, his parents despair that their son will ever grow up. Tom would dearly like to tell them all about everything he's done, and then they'd have a different idea about him. If only Dad could hear it straight from Bloomsbury or Russell how brave he'd been. If only Lady Caryatid could tell Mum what she'd said about him having wisdom beyond his years, then everything would be OK. But they'd never believe it from him. So he'll have to leave things as they are and accept that Mum and Dad have put him down as even less grown up than before.

To make matters worse, they now have a new concern about their son. They note that Tom has started daydreaming. They fear he will turn out just as vague and absent-minded as great-uncle Percy. For sometimes he has exactly the same misty, faraway look in his eyes. So perhaps putting the two of them together wasn't such a clever idea after all?

With regard to daydreaming, Tom's parents are right. For although they don't yet know it, their boy's head is full of the safari. In spirit he is already out there roaming the dunes. He has sand in his boots even before setting foot in the desert. He simply can't wait to see that magical sunrise on the Nile. There is only one small cloud on the horizon. Tom fears great-uncle Percy might easily forget to arrange the trip. So just to make quite sure he doesn't, he sends a steady stream of postcards to Professor Percival Parchment, Amnesia Cottage, Oblivion Avenue, Oxford.

www.ingramcontent.com/pod-product-compliance
Lightning Source LLC
Chambersburg PA
CBHW060356030726
47497CB00003B/741